**An ear-piercing**

He scanned the surro

A flash of pink punctuated the peaceful scene as it floated down the mountainside almost in slow motion. He'd recognize that bright pink anywhere.

"Nia?" he whispered and whipped out his binoculars to get a better look.

It was, in fact, Nia sliding down the mountainside.

He shoved the binoculars into his pack, strapped it across his shoulders and took off, strategizing the quickest way to get to her.

Why was she up here, anyway? Had something happened at the resort and she couldn't reach him by phone? He'd turned it off hoping for true solitude, thinking God could better hear his prayers if Aiden weren't distracted, because lately he'd felt abandoned by the Lord.

*Forget about that and get to Nia.*

An eternal optimist, **Hope White** was born and raised in the Midwest. She and her college sweetheart have been married for thirty years and are blessed with two wonderful sons, two feisty cats and a bossy border collie. When not dreaming up inspirational tales, Hope enjoys hiking, sipping tea with friends and going to the movies. She loves to hear from readers, who can contact her at hopewhiteauthor@gmail.com.

**Books by Hope White**

**Love Inspired Suspense**

### Echo Mountain

*Mountain Rescue*
*Covert Christmas*
*Payback*

*Hidden in Shadows*
*Witness on the Run*
*Christmas Haven*
*Small Town Protector*
*Safe Harbor*

Visit the Author Profile page at Harlequin.com.

# PAYBACK

## HOPE WHITE

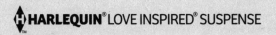

HARLEQUIN® LOVE INSPIRED® SUSPENSE

Recycling programs for this product may not exist in your area.

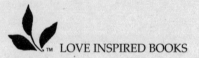

TM LOVE INSPIRED BOOKS

ISBN-13: 978-0-373-44675-9

Payback

www.Harlequin.com

Printed in U.S.A.

Greater love has no one than this:
to lay down one's life for one's friends.
–*John* 15:13

This book is dedicated to my wonderful Washington Family,
the Metters, Morins & Manns.

# ONE

She had to protect him.

Shivering against a strong gust of wind, Nia Sharpe quickened her pace up the mountain trail, determined to find her boss, resort manager Aiden McBride, by nightfall. She knew he was planning a midweek overnight hike to Pleasant Point and she needed to warn him.

Something didn't feel right about the two men, calling themselves Mark and Greg, who came looking for Aiden, men who claimed to be business associates. After they'd checked in, she had the resort's IT tech, Zack Carter, dig into their backgrounds, but he came up empty. It was as though the two men didn't exist.

As concierge for Echo Mountain Resort, it wasn't just Nia's job to help guests. She also prided herself on keeping Aiden's life as calm as possible.

When she'd learned that the mystery men rented hiking gear from the recreation office, her instincts went on full alert.

*Always trust your instincts.* A hard but valuable lesson she'd learned in childhood. One that she put to good use to protect her boss.

Fearing Mark and Greg had discovered Aiden's hiking plans by talking to resort staff, she took off at lunchtime to beat them to Pleasant Point.

She'd repeatedly called Aiden over the course of the past few hours, but he didn't answer. Reception was spotty in the mountains, so that was no surprise. A shudder trickled down her spine. Had the men already found Aiden?

Maybe she was overreacting, a force of habit from surviving an abusive household growing up. She also tended to overthink things where Aiden was concerned because she knew about the emotional trauma that had followed him home from the war. She seemed to be the only one.

"Miss Sharpe?"

She whipped around and spotted the two strangers heading up the trail. Had they followed her? Frustration ripped through her insides. If that was the case, she was leading them straight to Aiden.

*Play it cool, Nia.*

"What a coincidence finding you up here," the man calling himself Greg said. The obvious leader, he was tall and thin with a narrow face.

"Yes, indeed," Nia said as calmly as possible.

The men hesitated, as if they didn't want to scare her away.

"As long as we've run into you, could we ask you a few questions—" Greg hesitated "—about your boss?"

Mark, a husky, intense-looking man, watched her with assessing eyes.

"How about tomorrow at 9:00 a.m.?" she answered in the pleasant tone she used with guests. "I came out here for some peace and quiet. I'm sure you understand."

"How well do you know Aiden McBride?" Greg said, ignoring her request.

"As well as an employee knows her boss. Why?" She dug into her pocket for something she could use as a weapon. Her fingers wrapped around a cough drop. Great.

"We didn't want to announce this in a lobby full of people, but we're actually with the FBI. I'm Agent Greg Brown and this is Agent Mark McIntyre." Greg flashed what could be official ID; then again, maybe not.

"And you're interested in speaking with Mr. McBride? He's a war hero."

The men glanced at each other. "There's more to his

service record than has been made public," Greg said. "We could use your help with our investigation."

"Of course. I'll be in a better frame of mind to discuss this tomorrow during my shift." She smiled, her insides tangling into knots.

"Are you hiding something, Miss Sharpe?" Greg pressed.

"No, sir, but I do value my personal time."

Mark gave her a skeptical frown, and silence stretched between the three of them. Nia and Greg stared at each other, waiting for the other one to blink.

He took a step toward her.

She spun around and raced up the trail.

"Wait!" he called after her.

It was a good thing she loved to run, sometimes twice a day. Running kept her in good shape, although that wasn't why she did it. It calmed her mind and kept the dark memories at bay.

*Not a good time for a trip down memory lane, Nia.*

"Stop running!" Greg called after her.

Even if they were federal agents, they had no right to question her up here. She'd done nothing wrong and neither had Aiden. She was sure of it. Although a tough boss with a gruff exterior, Aiden was one of the kindest, most honorable men she'd ever known.

Aiden was also the first man who'd given her a chance. He truly respected her. She'd spent so many years attracting the same kind of man into her life: domineering, bullying men like her stepfather. Counseling and prayer had exposed that pattern, and she'd finally realized that subconsciously she thought that was how relationships—any relationships, romantic or not—were supposed to look.

At first she'd thought Aiden fit that same profile. But there was something different about him. She saw through his tough exterior and embraced a new kind of work relationship—one of trust and understanding. Which was why she had to find him, protect him.

She approached a switchback and adjusted her speed so she wouldn't lose her footing and go sailing over the sharp edge of the mountain. Out of the corner of her eye she spotted the men behind her, struggling to keep up. They were obviously not in shape to sprint uphill. She pumped harder, noticed a fork in the trail up ahead and decided to veer right. With any luck, her pursuers would take the other route.

Calming her mind, she focused on putting distance between herself and the men. She approached a clearing, the trail opening up to expose the valley below and a gorgeous vista of mountainous land. Suddenly something caught her eye.

Aiden?

Across the valley she spotted a bright yellow jacket, the one his sister Bree said could be seen from Mars. He must have changed his mind about camping overnight and decided to head back to the resort.

Which meant he was on a collision course with the agents.

"Aiden!" she called, waving her arms.

The enthusiastic movement threw her off balance and she stumbled. Trying to right herself, she skidded, flailing her arms to get her balance.

"Aiden!" she cried and slid over the edge.

An ear-piercing cry made Aiden freeze.

He scanned the surrounding area.

A flash of pink punctuated the peaceful scene as it floated down the mountainside almost in slow motion. He'd recognize that bright pink anywhere.

"Nia?" he whispered and whipped out his binoculars to get a better look.

It was, in fact, Nia sliding down the mountainside.

He shoved the binoculars into his pack, strapped it across his shoulders and took off, strategizing the quickest way to get to her.

Why was she up here, anyway? Had something happened at the resort and she couldn't reach him by phone? He'd turned it off hoping for true solitude, thinking God could better hear his prayers if Aiden wasn't distracted, because lately he'd felt abandoned by the Lord.

*Forget about that. Get to Nia.*

Nia, the incredibly efficient concierge who kept things running smoothly at the resort, especially on days Aiden was functioning at 30 percent.

She was also probably the one person who seemed to somehow know there was more to her boss than orders and demands, which was why he kept her at a safe distance. He felt exposed around her, vulnerable.

Right now she was the vulnerable one.

The splash of pink suddenly stopped. His gut tightened as he frantically searched the area above her, looking for the best way down. She'd landed at least five klicks away from a trail, so rappelling down would be the fastest way to get to her.

Crazed with worry, he slipped on the wet trail and scolded himself. He had to get his fear in check—fear of not being able to save her.

*Shake it off, McBride.*

Reeling in his erratic thoughts, he spotted the perfect location to anchor his rope. Within minutes he was there, securing the rope to a tree. Next, he created a classic rappel, using his body as a friction device. He straddled the rope, brought it around his right hip and across his chest, wrapped the rope over his left shoulder and across his back, then gripped the top end of the rope with his left hand and the bottom end with his right. The device wasn't pretty but it was functional.

"Nia!" he called.

Silence echoed back at him.

"Nia, I'm coming!" He hoped she was conscious but too stunned from her fall to answer.

He started down, pretending this was an emergency exercise, the kind that search-and-rescue team members practiced in case they lost their gear in the mountains but still had to complete a mission. As he descended to Nia's location, he felt the burn of rope rash across his body.

*Need to slow it down, get a grip on the panic.*

In his experience as a search-and-rescue, or SAR, member, he knew every minute was critical after a fall. As he edged his way down, he was glad he had a first-aid kit, water, extra food, rain gear and extra clothing with him. If Nia wasn't ambulatory they'd have to be rescued by Echo Mountain Search and Rescue, and it could take a few hours for the team to get to them.

A crack of thunder reverberated in the distance.

Aiden tried not letting the threat of an impending storm ruin his focus. He took a slow breath in through his nose and exhaled through his mouth. He had to be close.

"Aiden?"

His grip tightened on the rope. She was hurting, all right. He could hear it in her voice.

"Hang on, Nia," he said in what he hoped was a comforting tone.

He needed to get to her, save her. He wouldn't allow his own incompetence to cause him to lose another person he cared about.

He ventured a glance below and clenched his jaw at the sight of blood trailing down the side of Nia's face. Her big, brown eyes scanned her surroundings as if she wasn't quite sure how she'd ended up down there. She looked confused, as if she was suffering from a head injury.

"Nia, talk to me," he said, realizing he had farther to go than he'd originally thought.

"The men," she croaked.

"What men?" He lowered himself a few more inches.

"Two men checked in…looking for you."

She'd come out here to find Aiden and had been injured because of a work issue? Anger warred with worry. She shouldn't have risked her personal safety for her job. Could it be that her fear of Aiden's disappointment as a boss had driven her out here?

No, she was naturally and exceptionally efficient. He rarely had to offer constructive criticism because she was *that* good.

Maybe she excelled at her job, but she could use a tutorial in setting boundaries around her work. He was tempted to give her a quick lesson along with a stern lecture.

But if there was one thing he'd learned from his tumultuous relationship with his sister Bree, it was to tone down the domineering attitude when communicating with people. Sometimes he couldn't help himself, especially when he was consumed with worry.

He finally touched down and uncoiled the rope from his body. Dropping to his knees beside her, he said, "Are you okay?"

She nodded. "Yeah, yeah, I'm okay." She sat up.

"Whoa, take it easy."

"No, no time."

"I've got rain gear. We're okay."

"We have to go."

She was determined to get up, so he helped her. She put pressure on her left foot and winced.

"That's it. Back down you go." He adjusted her arm around his shoulders for support.

"We can't. Two men…they checked into the resort and I had to warn you—"

"It's just work, Nia. It could've waited until tomorrow."

It must have been his tone, because her eyes watered as he lowered her to the ground. Apparently he'd failed at softening his domineering tone.

Rather than say anything that might upset her further, he inspected her injury, a two-inch gash below the hairline on her forehead. It didn't look deep.

She sniffed and his insides coiled into a knot. Terrific.

He'd come down to rescue her and had only managed to cause more pain.

He wanted to apologize but didn't know how.

He dug the first-aid kit out of his pack. "So, you came out here to warn me about two particularly demanding guests?" he said in what he hoped was a teasing tone.

"They're federal agents."

Curious, but not alarmed, he pulled out antiseptic wipes and gauze. "Where else are you hurt besides your head injury and your ankle?"

"I'm fine. Patch me up so we can get out of here."

"Look, I know it's your nature to tend to everyone else's needs, but this time let me take care of you, okay?"

She gripped his arm. "They were determined to find you—"

"Well, I am the resort manager," he interrupted.

"They followed me up here and tried grilling me about you."

Okay, that was a little alarming, but he wouldn't let Nia see his worry. "Maybe they're working on a sensitive case."

He brushed antiseptic lotion against her wound and she winced.

"Sorry," he said.

"It's okay." She closed her eyes.

He hated that he was the one to inflict pain on such a lovely woman.

Lovely, intelligent, caring.

And completely out of his reach. Besides the fact that she was an employee, Aiden was in no position to explore a serious relationship, not until he unloaded some of his emotional baggage.

He'd never inflict that kind of angst on someone he cared about.

"Don't be angry with me," she said. "I was following my gut instincts."

"I'm not angry."

She raised an eyebrow.

"I guess my tone sounds angry. You should be used to that by now."

"It sounds edgier than usual," she said.

Of course it did. He was worried about Nia.

He finished dressing her head wound. "Okay, that's done."

She sat up again as if not wanting to appear weak. "Do you know your way down from here?"

"Yep, but you're not going anywhere on that bum ankle." He eyed the darkening sky. "I'll call it in."

"No, there's no time to wait for SAR."

"Hey, I've got everything we need to stay warm and dry."

"But the federal agents—"

"Are going to hightail it back down once they sense the storm's coming. Relax. It'll be okay."

He tried his cell phone but couldn't get a signal. Thankfully, he'd brought his radio.

"Base, this is Aiden, over." As he waited for a response from resort staff, he studied Nia. She looked younger in her hiking outfit, quite different than her office dress of dark suit and crisp white shirt.

"Why aren't they picking up?" she asked.

"Give them a minute," he said in a calm voice, to counterbalance her anxiety.

"Base, come in, over," he tried again.

A few tense seconds passed.

"Read you loud and clear, over," a voice finally answered.

"Harvey, is that you, over?" Aiden asked.

"Affirmative. I'm helping the new kid organize his marbles, over."

Aiden smiled to himself. Harvey, the resort's former security manager, was always the jokester, and Aiden appreciated him helping Scott, the new security manager, get acclimated.

"We have a situation," Aiden said. "Nia came looking for me and took a tumble."

"How serious, over?"

"I'm fine," Nia interjected as Aiden was about to answer. "Injured ankle, so she can't walk, over."

"You mean you can't carry her down by yourself, over?"

"Very funny, over."

"Give me your location, over."

Aiden dug out his topographical map and gave Harvey the coordinates.

"I'll contact the sheriff's department. There was a minor mud slide north of Rockland. I'm guessing most SAR volunteers are headed up there, over."

"Okay, keep me posted, over."

"Will do, over and out."

Aiden turned to Nia. "Let's get you comfortable."

"This is ridiculous. I can manage to walk down."

"And make your ankle worse? Not happening. I won't risk losing my best employee to bed rest because she aggravated her injury trying to hike down on a bum ankle."

She glanced away, her eyes drifting across the horizon.

*Way to go, McBride.* He knew he'd sounded concerned for her only as an employee, nothing more. Not what anyone wanted to hear. It wasn't true, but she could never know that.

"I'll set up shelter." He pulled equipment off his pack and got to work. It didn't make sense to pitch his small tent since the ground wasn't level and there was room for only one. Scanning his surroundings, Aiden figured out a way to anchor the tent fly to surrounding trees.

He was glad he had something to do to distract him from the cute brunette sitting a few feet away. He realized they'd never been alone together for more than a few minutes. They were always surrounded by people at the resort, either guests or employees, and Aiden made it a point to keep his distance from Nia outside of work.

"What if the agents find us?" Nia said softly.

"I doubt they're experienced enough to rappel down here," he offered.

He got the shelter up and helped her shift beneath it just as the rain started to fall.

"We've got a good sight line from here," he said. "Plus, the green tent fly offers good camouflage."

She sighed. "So, maybe the men won't see us."

He adjusted himself next to her, making sure their bodies didn't touch. "Why did they upset you so much?"

"People often are not what they seem," she said.

He wondered if she was talking about the agents or someone from her past. "You want to expand on that?"

"The men weren't forthcoming about who they really were when they checked in. Plus, they were trying to get me to say something bad about you."

"That shouldn't be too hard," he teased.

She glanced at him. "The one guy said there's more to your service record than has been made public. What did he mean?"

"I have no idea." And he didn't. Aiden had completed his tour of duty in an honorable fashion. Well, except for not being able to save Yates…

"What if they're not even federal agents?"

"Nia, don't let your imagination hijack your common sense. I'm sure it's nothing sinister."

The crack of a gunshot echoed across the mountains.

# TWO

"Aiden!" Nia cried, gripping his jacket and burying her face against his chest.

Aiden couldn't move for a second, the sound of gunfire paralyzing him. His heart pounding in his chest, he forced himself to take a shallow breath, then another. He gazed down at the top of Nia's head. She needed him to be strong, to be undamaged.

He would not let his trauma prevent him from easing her fear.

"I'll call it in," he said.

Nia's body trembled against him. He was torn between wanting to console her and being the soldier that could defend them against the enemy. Why would federal agents open fire on them?

"Hang on," he said. He took off his jacket and draped it around her shoulders, wanting to keep her warm and prevent her from going into shock. She leaned into him again, this time clinging to his sweatshirt. He clenched his jaw.

"Base, this is Aiden," he said into the radio. "We have an emergency, over."

Gunshots could sound close but originate from far away. It wouldn't surprise him if the shots came from idiots trying to hunt wild animals, or even a drug deal gone wrong. Everyone knew about the pot farms that occasionally sprang up in the most remote spots of the national park.

"This is Harvey, over."

"Our situation is serious, Harvey. We heard gunshots—"

"Someone's shooting at you, over?"

"Not sure if they're shooting at us, but they're definitively shooting at something, over."

"Permission to call in more employees so Scott and I can come out and get you ourselves, over?"

"Have Scott stay at the resort. See if you can get a sheriff's deputy to accompany you, over."

"But Scott is an ex-cop, over."

"Who's still recovering from recent trauma. I don't want to make that worse. See if you can track down Deputy Nate Walsh, over."

"Roger that. Stay safe, over."

Aiden clipped the radio to his belt. That was when he realized that although Nia clung to him, he wasn't returning the hug. He hadn't held a woman or comforted a woman since he'd returned from military service three years ago. As he tentatively slid his arm against her back, she pushed away from him.

"Sorry, sorry," she said.

"For what?"

Nia leveled him with tear-filled eyes. "It's inappropriate."

"To be scared?"

"You know what I mean."

"I'm not sure I do."

"I don't want to make this harder on you."

"Harder on me?"

"You've got a lot going on, trying to save me, the storm, the gunshots." She cast him a quick glance. "Are you… okay?"

His breath caught in his throat.

She knew.

Somehow Nia knew his deepest, darkest secret, the one he'd erroneously thought he'd expertly kept hidden from the world.

He ripped his gaze from her sweet brown eyes, ashamed that she knew how broken he was. She probably figured she didn't stand a chance of surviving out here with Aiden as her protector.

"I'm sorry," she repeated.

"Stop apologizing," he snapped. He didn't mean to sound so harsh, but it was his default when he came face-to-face with shame.

He grabbed his binoculars and shifted out from beneath the overhang into the rain. He didn't care about getting wet. He needed distance from Nia and to keep watch of the area for signs of trouble.

Slowly scanning the ridge to the left, he calmed his breathing and struggled to figure out how to apologize for his sharp tone. On the other hand, maybe she'd stop being so nice to him if he acted curt, because the nicer she was, the harder it would be for Aiden to stay on his side of the boss line.

As his eyes followed the trail to the south, he spotted two men hovering below. Could these be the men who were looking for Aiden? The men who had frightened Nia?

Aiden watched. Waited. The only weapon he had to defend him and Nia was his knowledge of wilderness survival and military training—training he had tried to forget.

A crack of ominous thunder made the two men look up at the sky. With a nod, the taller man motioned down the trail, back to civilization. They were headed out of the park, away from Nia and Aiden.

Nia shifted behind him, a whimper escaping her lips. His fingers clenched the binoculars. He desperately wanted to ease her pain.

"I'm sorry," he blurted out.

"What, they've found us?"

"No, I saw two men, but they're headed down."

"Oh, good."

He lowered the binoculars and turned to her but held his position outside the tent fly. "I'm apologizing for my tone just now."

"Oh, that." She waved her hand dismissively. "It's fine.

Come back under the shelter. I won't…you know, do anything that will make you uncomfortable."

Was that what she thought? That her touch made him uncomfortable? She couldn't be more off base. It wasn't that he was offended by her touch but that he ached for it. And that terrified him on so many levels.

"Please?" Nia said.

Aiden took a deep breath. He crawled under the tent fly and gripped the binoculars as a distraction, a way to break the tension between him and Nia.

Emotional tension.

Which was odd since he'd worked so hard to bottle up his emotions. It was the only way to prevent the shame from rising up and consuming him. He'd walled himself off.

Yet somehow Nia was standing right beside him, inside the fortress.

Out of the corner of his eye he saw her shivering again.

"Let's get you warm." He pulled a dark gray blanket out of his backpack.

When he turned to her, she glanced away, avoiding eye contact. He didn't blame her. He could be a real jerk. Hadn't his sister told him so on countless occasions?

He flung the blanket around her shoulders and pulled it together in front. "Hold it tight."

When she reached for the two ends, their fingers touched and a spark of warmth rushed up his arm. He snapped his hands back and shoved them into his pockets.

"Why did you decide not to camp at Pleasant Point?" she asked.

"I was stressing about the staff meeting tomorrow and wanted to get back."

She cracked a wry smile. "And you accuse me of being a workaholic. We had it all figured out."

"Base to Aiden, over," Harvey's voice called over the radio.

Aiden snapped the radio off his belt. "Go ahead, over."

"Nate, Will and I are on our way up with a litter to carry Nia back. It could take us an hour or two depending on the weather, over."

"We're not going anywhere, over."

"Any sign of the shooter, over?"

"Negative, although I spotted two men hiking down the South Ridge trail."

"Hang tight, over and out."

Aiden clipped the radio to his belt.

"Do you think they'll get here in time?" Nia said.

"In time for what?"

"Before the agents find us?"

"Nia—" he took one of her hands in his, surprised by his own action "—the two men headed back down were probably the agents. Besides, if they need to question me, they wouldn't want to shoot me, right?"

She nodded but didn't look convinced.

"Maybe they felt threatened by a wild animal and fired off a shot to scare it away," he said.

"I guess that's possible." She nibbled at her lower lip and glanced down.

"Hey, look at me." He would have tipped her chin to look into his eyes, but he was already touching her hand and couldn't risk an even more intimate touch. "Nia? What is it about these men that terrified you so much?"

She looked up. "I don't trust them."

"Just federal agents, or law enforcement in general?"

"Busted," she said softly.

"You want to tell me why you have a thing against police officers?"

She shrugged. A few seconds passed. He would not push her.

"My stepfather was a cop and…" Her voice trailed off. She released a huge breath. "He wasn't a very nice guy. Then there was the cop that arrested my little brother." She shook her head. "They planted drugs on Danny to manipulate him into helping them nail a drug dealer. I guess you could say I haven't had the greatest experiences with cops."

"I'm sorry."

She shrugged. "I've been praying for God to open my heart so I wouldn't be prejudiced against *all* cops, and it's helped. But when the FBI agents came looking for you, my protective instincts overruled my compassion, I guess."

"At least God hears you," he let slip.

"I'm sorry?" She frowned as if she didn't understand his words.

"Nothing."

"God hears us all, Aiden."

"Or maybe some of us aren't worth His effort." He wanted to yank the words back, but they were out there, exposed for Nia to analyze.

Instead of responding with some trite comment, she placed her hand on top of his and offered a warm smile. "Would you mind if I lay down until the team gets here?"

"You trust me to keep watch?"

"Completely."

Nia didn't pursue Aiden's comment about not being worth God's attention. Arguing theology wasn't the way she wanted to pass the time while they awaited rescue. Besides, she knew his words were born of emotional trauma from the war. Eventually God would heal that, too.

She decided to cherish her time alone with Aiden, time she'd probably never experience again. Aiden was a master at keeping his distance from Nia. She used to think he didn't like her. But that couldn't be it. After all, he'd hired her. Sure, he'd hired her for her professionalism, and organizational and customer-service skills. Nothing more.

But she thought it odd that they rarely spent more than a few minutes alone together at work, and never outside work. They were always surrounded by people at various employee functions. Even at his mom's Christmas open house, they were crowded into a room full of neighbors and church friends.

The only time they'd been alone was the day she'd heard him cry out in pain and went to investigate, the day she'd spied through his bedroom window and watched him writhe in emotional pain, calling out a name: *Yates*.

She'd wanted to snap him out of the terrorizing nightmare and pounded on his front door to interrupt the torture. When he opened it, he stood there for a good five seconds, looking at Nia as if he didn't recognize her. His shirt was soaked with sweat and his eyes were bloodshot.

That was the moment in which she'd realized Aiden's gruffness was a cover for something else. Her heart ached for him, and she'd abandoned thoughts of quitting her job because she'd thought she'd fallen into a familiar pattern of working with another domineering male.

At that moment she'd wanted so desperately to ease his pain, go inside his cottage and make him a hot cup of green tea. But instinct warned her not to let on she knew the truth, so she made up some lame excuse for knocking on the door, politely excused herself and took off.

As she lay beside him studying his strong profile, Nia took comfort in the fact that he was determined to protect her, even though she sensed he didn't think himself up to the task.

What had happened in Iraq that haunted him so?

She considered the agent's comment about there being more to Aiden's service record than was made public. Had whatever traumatized Aiden caught up to him? If that was the case, she'd better sharpen her observation skills and respect her intuition even more in order to protect him.

Protect him? How was she going to do that when she couldn't even walk? She yawned, realizing the adrenaline rush must have worn off because she was suddenly exhausted. She forced her eyes open, fighting sleep, but her eyelids fluttered shut again.

As random thoughts drifted across her mind, she could have sworn she felt Aiden gently touching her forehead. Maybe it was a dream, or maybe it was real. She felt grounded when he was near, even if he didn't seem to want to touch her, like before, when the gunshot echoed across the mountains and she'd thrown herself into his arms.

Talk about a dumb move. It obviously made him uneasy, which was the last thing she wanted to do. Yet only a minute ago he'd held her hand so gently. She could still feel the warmth from his touch, a touch that lit her insides.

*Get a grip, Nia. This is your boss, not your boyfriend.*

Nor could he be anything more than her boss. He'd made it clear on many occasions that his plate was full with work and family. Romance was not in his future.

Romance, something Nia ached for yet wouldn't risk with just any man, especially after her dismal track record of picking the absolute wrong men to spend time with.

The sound of rain tapping against the tent fly relaxed her even more. She drifted off into a lovely daydream about she and Aiden taking a boat out onto Lake Hawthorne, warmed by the sunshine as they enjoyed the subtle, rhythmic movement against the calm waters. They held hands, shared secrets and even laughed.

Suddenly a large speedboat headed in their direction, aiming right for them. Grabbing the oars, they tried to paddle away but weren't fast enough. The speedboat was barreling down on them…

"Nia!"

She gasped, opening her eyes. Aiden's handsome face stared down at her.

"They're here," he said.

"Who…what?"

"Harvey and his team, remember?"

"Oh, right." She sat up.

"You okay?" he asked.

"Sure."

"Bad dream?"

"Yep."

Because she feared that the boat in her dream represented the ultimate destruction of anything good in her life.

And in this case, anything she could share with Aiden.

Later that evening, Nia was embarrassed by all the attention she was getting, especially from Aiden. He hadn't left her side since they brought her down from the mountain. Aiden stayed close at the hospital, questioning medical staff about Nia's injuries and course of treatment.

She was amazed that Aiden had hung around for five hours until she was discharged. She told him to drop her off at her apartment in town, but he said he had something to pick up at the resort. It turned out to be a care package assembled by Bree, who was on the SAR K9 team, and other SAR friends. Some of them were waiting for her there, including Aiden's sister and her boyfriend, Scott, the resort's new security manager, along with Grace, head of the SAR K9 team, and the three men who'd rescued her this afternoon: Harvey, Nate and Will Rankin, a young widower with two little girls.

As Nia sat in the employee lounge with her wrapped, sprained ankle up on a chair, the group discussed the day's events.

"It's a good thing your injuries weren't serious," Will said. "That was quite a drop."

"In case I forgot to say it before, thank you for coming to get me." She nodded at Harvey, Nate and Will. Nia felt especially bad that she'd put Will in danger considering he was sole parent to his two girls.

"I'm glad I could be there," Will said. "You were there plenty of times for me."

After Will's wife passed away from cancer, Nia had joined a group of ladies from church who'd made it their goal to help Will through the darkness of grief. They'd brought him food, run errands and even held special prayer meetings.

"I've made some inquiries about the agents who followed you into the mountains," Deputy Nate Walsh said. "I hope to hear back tomorrow."

"Did they come back down the mountain?" Nia said.

"No one's seen them since they left on their hike this afternoon."

"Do you think they ran into trouble out there?" Grace asked.

"Maybe they left town," Aiden offered from the corner of the lounge.

Nia suspected his comment was meant to ease her worry.

"I don't get why they followed you up there in the first place," Bree chimed in.

"They were determined to talk to me about my boss."

"You're sure they were federal agents?" Scott asked.

"They flashed ID."

"What I don't get is—"

"Enough," Aiden interrupted his sister. "Nia needs a break from all the questions."

"Why, so she can get back to work?" Bree teased.

"Always busting my chops," Aiden muttered. "Don't you have to get some sleep so you can be up with the sun to plant rhodies on Overlook Drive?"

"I can function on very little sleep." Bree crossed her arms over her chest.

Bree and Aiden had an interesting relationship, Nia mused. They poked and prodded one another and loved each other dearly.

"I'd better get going," Will said. "Call if you need anything, Nia."

"Thanks. Hug the girls for me."

"You bet." Will nodded at the group and left.

"Come on, sweetheart, I'll walk you back to the cottage," Scott said to Bree.

Bree gave Nia a hug. "We're so glad you're okay." Bree glanced at Aiden. "Right, big brother?"

"Of course. This place would fall apart without her," Aiden said.

Bree shook her head.

"What?" Aiden said.

"It's always about work with you."

"Hey, what's the update on the mud slide victims?" Nia asked.

"No fatalities and everyone is accounted for," Scott said.

"Praise God," Grace said.

A moment of contemplative silence blanketed the room.

"Well, keep that ankle elevated," Bree said.

"Will do, thanks."

Bree took Scott's hand and they left the lounge.

"I'd better be going, too." Grace grabbed her purse.

"I'll see you to your car," Harvey said. He cast a quick glance at Nia. "Buddy system, got it?"

"I know, I know. Next time I won't go hiking without a buddy."

Aiden's phone buzzed. "This is Aiden…Uh-huh. Sure, that's fine."

But by the tone of his voice, Nia could tell it wasn't fine. He shoved the phone into his pocket.

"What's wrong?" Nia asked Aiden.

"Nothing you need to think about. Let's get you home."

"Can I help?" Harvey offered.

"Nope, it's all good." Aiden extended his hand to Nia. "Ready?"

"I can give her a ride," Grace offered.

"Thanks, but I'm her boss. I feel responsible for her."

Right, her boss, not her friend, nor her boyfriend. He had to suspect she cared about him more than she should; therefore, he felt it necessary to make the boundary clear.

She ignored his hand and stood.

"Hey, hey." Aiden shoved the crutches at her.

"It's not that bad."

"Let's keep it from getting worse."

She adjusted them under her armpits. Trying to get her balance, she wobbled and Aiden gripped her arm to keep her steady.

A flush crept up her cheeks. She was *so* not the helpless waif she seemed to be at this moment.

"I'm not used to these things," she said.

"Give it time," Aiden encouraged her.

She got her balance and glanced into his eyes. "I'm good. You can…" She nodded at his hand.

His fingers sprang free of her arm. "Right, sorry. I'll grab the care package."

Even with the basket of goodies in his arms, he managed to open every door for her as they headed to his car.

"My car. How will I—"

"Bree and I will bring it by tomorrow," he said.

"Or maybe I can have my neighbor drive me to the resort."

"I meant it when I said you should stay home, take it easy."

"Okay, boss." She wondered if she'd made him so uncomfortable this afternoon that he didn't want her around.

She was thinking too much and it was giving her a headache. Once inside his truck, she buckled up and rested her head against the seat. The day's events caught up to her in a big way. With a sigh, she closed her eyes.

Aiden got behind the wheel and clicked the radio on low to a classical station. She'd never pegged him as a classical-music fan.

She let the sounds of string instruments wash over her, pushing aside fear and anxiety about the day's events.

"Nia?"

She opened her eyes. They were parked in front of her apartment. "Wow, that was fast."

"You were out that whole time? That doesn't seem right. Maybe we should call the doctor."

"Aiden, stop fretting. I'm exhausted and I'm the type that can fall asleep like that." She snapped her fingers. "Nothing to worry about."

She opened her door, but by the time she got the tips of her crutches on the ground, Aiden was there, offering his assistance. She cracked a half smile. "Thanks, but I'm good."

He grabbed the basket from the backseat and escorted her to the building.

"Thanks again for staying with me at the hospital. I really need to go online and give you a five-out-of-five star review as a boss."

"Yeah, right," he said with an edge of sarcasm to his voice. "Keys?" He extended his hand and she plopped them into his palm.

Holding the basket in one hand, he managed to unlock the door with the other. As he swung it wide, she realized he'd never been inside her home.

"You may set the basket on the dining room table," she said, cringing at the sight of her messy living room.

He slid the basket onto the table and went into the kitchen.

"What are you—"

"Making you an ice bag for the ankle."

She listened to him search her cabinets for a plastic bag, then dig in her freezer for ice. She wanted to tell him to stop, that she could take care of herself, but didn't want to seem rude.

He returned to the living room with the ice bag. "You want to lie down?"

"I got it, thanks." She put her hand out and he gave her the ice.

"You can manage carrying—"

"I'm fine."

With a nod, he headed for the door. "I'll wait in the truck until I see your lights go out and I know you're asleep."

"That's really not necessary."

"Nia." He pinned her with those striking blue eyes of his. "This is not a negotiation."

"Well, it shouldn't take long. I'll probably flop down on the bed and fall asleep in my clothes."

"As long as you get a good night's sleep. I'll check in tomorrow."

With a nod, he shut the door. Nia exhaled a gasp of air. She'd been holding her breath. Why, because she desperately wanted his approval of her apartment? She shook her head.

She was tempted to turn off the lights to release him from his duties, but she knew he wouldn't buy it. Hobbling down the hall, she flipped on the bedroom light, tossed the ice bag on the bed and went back to turn off the living room lights.

She leaned the crutches against the bathroom wall and washed her face. The ankle wasn't extremely painful, which was good. Of course, Aiden was right. Icing it would make it feel even better.

The sound of a barking dog echoed through her closed window. It reminded her of Bree and members of the SAR team who'd rallied around her at the resort. It felt so good to have friends. It had taken Nia more than seven years and multiple moves before she'd felt at home and connected to people.

She made her way to the bedroom and leaned the crutches against her nightstand. She turned off the bedside lamp and flopped down, so very glad to be in her own bed. The full moon illuminated her room through the sheer curtains.

She casually flung the comforter over her body and said a quick prayer, giving thanks that her injuries had been minor and that both she and Aiden were safe.

A thud echoed from the living room.

Nia jackknifed in bed. Had she imagined it?

Silence rang in her ears as she strained to listen.

Another thud followed by a crash made her grab her cell

phone and dive out of bed. She scrambled behind her reading chair in the corner and dialed 911.

*Be calm. Tamp down the adrenaline rush. Use your head.*

"Nine-one-one emergency," the operator answered.

"There's someone in my apartment," Nia whispered.

Footsteps pounded into her room.

# THREE

She held her breath, tensing every muscle in her body against the anticipated assault of a stranger.

Silence filled the room. She swallowed back her terror. "Nia?"

She peeked around the chair, recognizing her brother's profile. "Danny?"

He eyed her. "What are you doing back there?"

"Ma'am, we're sending an officer to—"

"No, it's okay," Nia interrupted the 911 operator. "It's my brother."

More footsteps pounded into the room. Someone launched himself at Danny.

Aiden.

"Wait, Aiden!" she cried.

Aiden whipped Danny to the floor and pinned him with a knee against his back.

"Call 911!" he ordered.

She clicked on the bedside lamp. "Aiden, it's okay. It's my brother."

Aiden had that look in his eyes, as if he was someplace else and couldn't hear her. His brain must be pickled in adrenaline. As Danny struggled against Aiden's hold, Nia crawled across the bedroom and placed a calming hand on Aiden's back.

He snapped his attention to her, his eyes ablaze.

"It's okay," she said. "That's my brother, Danny."

Aiden glanced down at Danny, then back at Nia. "Your brother?"

Nia nodded. "Yes. Everything's okay."

Danny squirmed. "Get off me."

Aiden shifted off him and stood. She noticed his hands were trembling.

The last thing Nia wanted was to cause more trauma, and she certainly didn't want Aiden feeling embarrassed about protecting her. But the truth was, she hadn't seen Danny in three years, and he didn't have a key to her place, which meant he'd broken in. He must be desperate. She hoped he was here to see her, not to steal something to pawn.

*Nia, that's a horrible thing to think.* Yet, with his track record, she couldn't help but go there.

Aiden got Nia's crutches and offered them to her. "Sorry," he told Danny.

"You should be, jerk." Danny got to his feet and gripped his side. "I think I cracked a rib."

"Let's go into the living room," Nia said, motioning them ahead of her.

Her twenty-four-year-old brother stormed out of the bedroom. Nia sensed Aiden was about to apologize again, so she stopped him. "Thank you for protecting me."

"What's your relationship with your brother like?" Aiden said.

"We don't talk much. We're not close." She hobbled across the bedroom.

"But he has a key to your place?"

As she struggled to come up with an answer that wouldn't upset Aiden further, her brother called from the kitchen, "You got anything stronger than lemonade?"

"No, Danny, I don't *have* anything stronger than lemonade."

He shut the refrigerator and joined them in the living room. He hadn't changed much, still wearing his favorite Detroit Lions jacket and cowboy boots.

"I could use a beer," he said.

"And I could use an explanation." She shifted onto the couch.

"I haven't heard from you in years and suddenly you show up in my apartment late at night? Are you in trouble again?"

"Me? Of course not," he said in a charming voice.

She disliked that tone. It made her wonder if everything he said was a lie.

"So introduce me to your boyfriend." Danny sized up Aiden, who hovered near the bookshelves, arms crossed over his chest.

"He's not my boyfriend. He's my boss."

"Yeah, right, and what, he was bringing by paperwork at—" Danny checked his phone "—eleven-fifteen?"

"It's been a long day," she said. "I was in a hiking accident and Aiden brought me home from the hospital. It's late and I'm tired. What can I do for you?"

"What can you do for me? Whoa, you make it sound like I'm a customer or something. Ya know what, never mind." He started for the door.

Guilt snagged her conscience. "Hey, come on. Don't leave."

He hesitated and turned to her. "Sorry I bothered you."

"It's not a bother, but your timing couldn't be worse, that's all. Come on, sit down." She patted the sofa next to her.

He glanced across the room at Aiden but didn't move. She sensed her boss intimidated her brother.

"Aiden, it's okay," she said. "I need a little alone time with my brother."

"Are you sure?"

"Yes, I'll be fine."

Aiden pushed away from the wall and crossed the room. Stopping in front of Danny, he said, "She needs to rest."

Danny offered a mock salute. "Aye, aye, Captain."

Aiden cast one last glance at Nia. "I'll be outside in the car if you need me."

"No, really, go home. It's all good."

Aiden brushed past Danny as if he didn't exist and closed the door.

"Whoa, sis, you really know how to pick 'em." Danny went to her bookshelves and fingered a framed picture she'd taken on a recent hike at Echo Mountain. "What's this?"

"Spruce Falls. Danny, why are you—"

"Is it hard to get to?"

"Not too hard. It's off the main trail up to the summit."

"It looks…peaceful—" he hesitated "—safe, like you could hide up there and no one would find you."

*Not even the stepmonster.* She heard the inference about Walter, their stepfather. Feeling safe was something both she and Danny craved with every fiber of their being.

He glanced at her. "Maybe you'll take me there someday?"

"Sure."

"But leave the intense boyfriend home."

"Again, he's my boss, not my boyfriend, and he has every right to be intense. You broke into my apartment. What's that about?"

He hung his head and wandered toward the sofa. "Sorry, I didn't want to wake you."

"Try again."

He shrugged. "I was afraid you wouldn't let me in."

"When have I ever turned you away, little brother?"

"You haven't, but I figured you would eventually."

"Danny, what's going on?" she said with worry in her voice. She tried keeping the judgment in check.

"I needed a break from working in the shop."

"You're still working on cars?" she said, hopeful. That meant he wasn't involved in something illegal.

"I was, until a few months ago. Decided to try something else, but it didn't work out and the guy in charge is kinda upset with me, so I thought I'd get away and come visit my sister." He shot her that killer smile, the one she suspected blinded the ladies.

Nia wasn't falling for it. "What was the *something else*?"

"Huh?"

"The other job you took after leaving the garage?"

"Collections."

"What kind of collections?"

"What, you don't trust me?"

"Danny," she pressed.

He turned away and paced the living room. "I worked for a guy who loaned money to people and I collected."

"And where did he get this money that he so generously loaned out?"

"I don't know."

"Maybe you should leave."

Danny looked at her in shock. "What?"

"I want the truth. That's all I've ever asked of you. What was the guy into?"

"I don't know, Nia. Honest."

"Drugs? Was he a drug dealer?"

"Why do you always go to that place? You know I was set up when I was a kid."

"I'm sorry, but you haven't made the best decisions in the past."

"I'm trying to get my life together, and maybe I shouldn't have taken this collections gig, but I'm out now. I want to find something steady."

"In Echo Mountain?" she said, trying to tamp down her panic.

Although she loved her brother, she suspected he wasn't serious about straightening out his life, and he usually brought trouble with him wherever he went.

"Obviously the thought freaks you, so I guess not."

Once again, the guilt anchor pulled her down. If only she'd been a better sister...

"I'm sorry," she said. "But I never know what you're going to get into next."

She'd finally made a stable life for herself in Echo Mountain, a life blessed with generous and loving friends.

"I came here because I needed your help," he said.

She held her breath.

"But you've obviously given up on me," he whispered.

"Stop talking like that. What do you need?"

"A place to lie low for a few weeks, maybe even a job. What about at the resort? They've got to have something there for me."

Her instincts piqued. "Daniel, why do you need to 'lie low.'"

"I sorta lost some of my boss's money."

"What do you mean lost it?"

"It was a good deal, guaranteed to double my money and—"

"You gambled it away?"

"It was a sure thing. The guy gave me—"

Nia put up her hand. "I don't want to know the details. How much did you lose?"

He hesitated before answering. "Two grand. I figured I could get a job and save everything I made if I moved in with you, and pay the guy off in a few months."

A shudder ran down her spine. She loved her brother, but neither loved nor trusted his decisions. If he applied for a job at Echo Mountain resort, they'd do a background check and discover his criminal record.

And her shame.

"You're welcome to spend the night." Nia grabbed her crutches and stood. "There's an extra pillow and blanket in the front closet. You have a car, right?"

"Sure."

"Tomorrow morning you can take me to the bank and I'll withdraw money from my savings so you can pay off your boss."

"No, Nia—"

"Danny, you're my brother and I want to help, but this is the last time, okay?"

"Yeah, thanks, sis."

Nia went into her bedroom and shut the door. She couldn't take one more random thing today: the federal agents looking for Aiden, her terrifying fall and now her estranged brother showing up—make that breaking into her apartment—and asking for help. Worse, he suggested he insinuate himself into her carefully arranged life. She loved him, but nothing good could come of that.

She fought a sudden headache and collapsed on the bed. Glancing out the window, she noticed Aiden's car parked across the street. The inside light was on and it looked as if he was reading something.

She should call him, tell him she was fine and he was relieved of his duties, yet she took comfort in knowing he was watching over her.

Since escaping her abusive stepfather, Nia had always prided herself on being a self-sufficient, strong woman who'd left her hardships behind. It all seemed to come rushing back with the appearance of her brother, the boy she'd tried to protect.

She should feel content that Danny was in the next room and Aiden was outside. Instead, she was still rattled from the afternoon's events and felt a bit off center. She took a deep breath and recited one of her favorite passages from the Bible, Psalm 138:7.

"'Though I walk in the midst of trouble, you preserve my life,'" she whispered. "'You stretch out your hand against the anger of my foes; with your right hand you save me.'"

*One more. They had one more building to check.*

*Aiden collapsed on the hard earth, gripping his leg. He wasn't sure he'd make it.*

*"You okay, Mac?" his friend, twenty-year-old Buddy Yates, said.*

*"Football injury acting up. I'm fine." Aiden tried to stand and the knee gave out again.*

*"Yeah, not so fine," Yates said. "Hang back."*

*Aiden wanted to argue but knew he'd only slow down the process if he hobbled along, and they all wanted to get back to base ASAP.*

*"Be right back, old man." Yates shot Aiden that goofy smile and walked away.*

*An explosion rocked the ground, debris flying everywhere, a wall of dust blocking visibility.*

*"Yates!" Aiden called out.*

*"I'm good!"*

*A barrage of gunfire echoed across the small village.*

*"Yates!"*

He gasped and opened his eyes, glancing around in confusion, trying to figure out where he was. Gripping the steering wheel, he realized he sat in his truck back in Echo County, Washington. He wasn't in the sandbox.

Someone tapped on his window and he snapped his head to the left. Nia frowned at him from the other side of the glass. He counted to three, struggling to get a grip.

He lowered the window. "Good morning," he said, but even he could tell his voice didn't sound right.

"Want some coffee?" Nia handed him a travel mug. "Black with two sugars, right?"

"What time is it?"

"Nearly ten. I can't believe you stayed here all night."

He couldn't believe she was making small talk after just witnessing his pure and utter weakness. The nightmares were less frequent lately but no less terrifying.

They had to stop.

He took the coffee and their hands touched. In the briefest of seconds that connection drove away the brutal images that terrorized him in his sleep.

"Thanks," he said.

"Why didn't you go back to the resort last night?" she asked, leaning on a crutch.

"Guess I fell asleep." Which was true. He could have left, but there'd been something about her brother that didn't sit right with Aiden. "Where's your other crutch?"

"Inside. I only need one."

"Nia," he said in warning.

"You must be sore from sleeping in your truck. Want to come in?"

"Don't change the subject. You need to use both crutches."

"Fine, come in and have breakfast."

He eyed her building. "Is your brother...?"

"Still asleep."

"No, thanks. Wouldn't want to wake him."

She glanced down for a second, then pinned him with soft brown eyes. "I'm sorry that you and Danny got into it. He didn't—" she hesitated "—hurt you, did he?"

"Hey, I was the one who had him pinned, remember?" he teased.

But they both knew she wasn't referring to physical injuries. Which meant she'd sensed the physical altercation had set off his posttraumatic nightmare.

"I know, but I wish it hadn't happened," she said.

He didn't want her feeling responsible for his problem. "You and your brother work things out last night?"

"More or less. I'm not sure we'll ever completely work things out. It's a complicated relationship."

"Aren't they all."

His cell vibrated. "McBride," he answered.

"You okay, boss?" Scott asked. "You didn't come back last night."

"I was watching over Nia."

"Okay, well, what do you want me to tell employees about the staff meeting?"

"Ah, right, the staff meeting."

"That's this morning," Nia said, panicked.

"Sorry, Scott," Aiden said into the phone. "I guess with everything that happened yesterday, I lost track of things. We can reschedule—"

"No," Nia interrupted. "It was a major hassle getting everyone's schedules worked out so we could meet. Tell them we'll be there in twenty minutes."

"We?"

"Sure. I'm coming with you."

He read determination and something else in her eyes, something he'd never seen before. A softness when she looked at him.

"Nia, you're supposed to take it easy. We'll manage."

"I need to be there. Be right back." She headed to her building barely using the one crutch.

Aiden wanted her to stay home and take care of herself, not come to work. Then again, maybe work would keep her mind occupied and off the events of the past eighteen hours.

"Boss?" Scott said.

"Tell everyone to assemble in the barn in twenty."

"Will do. How's Nia?"

"She seems okay."

"Is she still standing beside you?"

"No. Why?"

"Deputy Walsh wasn't able to confirm the two men looking for you were federal agents," Scott said. "They could be undercover and using aliases. With your permission I'd like to do a little digging of my own."

"Sure. Go for it."

"Okay, see you when you get here."

"Thanks." Aiden pocketed his phone and considered that bit of information. If the guys weren't federal agents, who were they and what did they want with him?

One thing for sure: Nia's instincts had been on the mark. Those men weren't who they said they were. She had never spoken much about her past, and Aiden wondered if her childhood had been a violent one that she'd rather not relive. Maybe that was why she didn't ask him about his own trauma: because she'd felt the same type of shame, the kind you felt when trauma consumed you.

Nia couldn't have experienced the level of trauma that Aiden battled—at least, he hoped she hadn't. No one should be saddled with the kind of guilt that weighed down his heart each and every day: guilt about the last time he spoke to his father before his death; guilt about Yates dying right in front of him; and even guilt about not being able to protect Bree from an abusive ex-boyfriend.

Aiden had gone nearly a month without nightmares and he'd hoped he might be past all that. Apparently last night's hand-to-hand combat with Nia's brother ignited the trauma.

Whipping open the door, he stepped out of the truck and stretched his arms over his head. He glanced at her apartment window, imagining her deadbeat brother passed out on the couch. Aiden was pretty sure that guy didn't have Nia's best interests at heart.

But Aiden did. She'd done so much for him, and not just as the resort's concierge.

He wasn't sure how he was going to maintain his distance since he'd have to stay close to protect her, but somehow he'd manage. He had to fortify that boundary in order to keep his perspective. Emotions made you weak and sloppy, and he couldn't afford to be either if he was going to keep her safe.

Aiden kept the meeting short, mostly because he wanted to get Nia back home with her ankle elevated. It was obvious the woman didn't know the meaning of the word *relax* as she darted here and there on one crutch, passing out materials and making sure everyone had a beverage. It was as if she was playing hostess. Aiden mused she'd make a great hostess, and a wonderful wife someday.

*Whoa, watch it, buddy.*

An hour later the meeting ended and a few people approached Nia, asking about her fall and subsequent injuries.

"So, nothing serious?" Tripp, the front-desk associate, asked.

"A minor head cut and sprained ankle. I'm really fine."

"Are you taking time off?" Tripp said.

"I don't plan to."

"That decision is up to her boss," Aiden chimed in. "And he'd feel better if Nia took the necessary time off to nurse her injuries."

"Interesting how you're referring to yourself in the third person, big brother," Bree said with a raised eyebrow.

"Like that, huh?" Aiden countered. He didn't want to argue with his sister today. He simply didn't have the energy after his mostly sleepless night.

"Thanks, everyone. Back to work," Aiden ordered.

Nia started for her office.

"Nia, you should—"

"Come on, boss," she interrupted. "At least let me go through my inbox."

"Okay, if you wrap it up by one."

"Deal." She left the barn and Aiden followed.

Scott approached Aiden. "We've got an issue with the pool-access door. Key cards are sporadically not working."

"That's why I hired the new tech."

"Carter's on it, but I thought you should know."

"How long has this been going on?"

"A day, maybe two."

"He needs to speed things up." Aiden glanced around and lowered his voice. "Anything more on the federal agents?"

"No, sir. I've got some feelers out." They entered the resort's main lodge. Scott hesitated by his office. "We'll figure it out."

Aiden's gaze wandered to Nia as she turned the corner.

"You're worried about her," Scott said.

"She could have been seriously injured yesterday."

"Why do I sense there's something else?"

Aiden glanced at Scott. "Her estranged brother showed up out of the blue last night. He and I got into it."

"Estranged as in...?"

"I don't know yet. Wouldn't surprise me if he's into something criminal. He gives off that vibe."

"Want me to..."

"Yeah, check him out. Danny, or Daniel Sharpe."

"You think he's dangerous?"

"I do. He's got a solid left hook and a cocky attitude."

"Aiden!" Nia screamed.

# FOUR

Aiden raced toward the sound, his heart pounding against his chest. How could Nia be in danger at the resort surrounded by all these people?

He rushed into the doorway of her office and froze. She stood beside her desk, hands cupping her cheeks. It looked as if a tornado had whipped through her office. Papers littered her desk and the floor, a chair was upside down, and a blue glass vase was in pieces by the window.

He calmed his breathing. She was okay. No one had hurt her.

Scott hovered beside Aiden. He sensed a small group of employees forming in the hallway.

He didn't take his eyes off Nia. "Everyone, back to work," he said.

Wearing a puzzled frown, she leaned against her desk while plucking a few pieces of paper off the top.

"I don't understand," she said. "Who would do this?"

Aiden glanced at Scott. "Call Echo Mountain PD to report the break-in, check surveillance video from the last twelve hours and keep digging into those federal agents."

"Yes, sir."

Aiden stepped into Nia's office and shut the door.

Nia glanced at the floor where a figurine lay broken in half. It was a delicate woman with her hands pressed together in prayer.

"My Peace figurine." She started to kneel down, but he put out his hand.

"I've got it." Aiden picked up the two pieces and analyzed them. "A little superglue and she'll be as good as new. I keep some in my office."

She eyed the broken figurine in his hand. "Thanks."

A lost expression settled across her features. He wanted to take her in his arms and tell her everything would be okay. Instead, he plucked a table lamp off the floor and placed it on her credenza.

"I don't get it," she said. "There's nothing worth stealing except my computer and it's still here. How did someone ransack my office without anyone hearing it?"

"Must have happened in the middle of the night when this part of the building is empty. Front-desk personnel are too far away to hear anything."

"You think it was the federal agents looking for information on you?"

"We're not even sure those men are legitimate federal agents."

"Well, whoever they are, they're exceptionally skilled if they can get into my locked office without being noticed." She shuddered.

"We shouldn't assume this was a targeted break-in," Aiden offered, grabbing a stapler and file tray off the floor. He slid them onto her paper-covered desk.

"This is a mess. I need to—"

"No, you don't. This office is off-limits until we speak with the authorities. They might decide to dust for prints."

"Oh, okay," she said, as if the mention of authorities made everything worse.

Someone had been rifling through her things. Looking for what?

That was the part that plagued Aiden. The perpetrator obviously thought Nia had access to important documents worth breaking the law for. The next question was, were they worth hurting someone over?

He needed to keep an eye on Nia, at least until they figured out who ransacked her office.

"Is anything missing?" he asked.

"I don't think so. But it's hard to tell." Her brows furrowed in a look of devastation.

He couldn't stand it. Aiden put his arm around her and pulled her against his chest. He thought he was doing this right; he hoped he was doing it right. She slid one arm around his waist and squeezed, returning the hug.

Stroking her back, he said, "It'll be okay."

They stood there for a good minute and he realized how utterly normal it felt to be holding her, comforting her.

Suddenly she pushed away. "Of course it will be okay. I'm being overly dramatic, sorry." Stepping away without using her crutches, she opened her office door. "Can I check my email from your office?"

"Not unless you take these." He grabbed the crutches and handed them to her.

"Fine," she said and headed into the hallway.

His heart still pounding from the hug, he followed close behind her.

Then he had a horrible thought: What if his office had been broken into, as well?

"Hang on," he said, touching her shoulder. "Let me go in first."

He walked ahead of her and his phone buzzed. He ripped it off his belt. "McBride."

"What's going on?" his sister said. "I see police cars out front."

"Someone broke into Nia's office."

"What? Why?"

"Not sure."

"Should I come back to be with Nia?"

"No, finish planting the rhodies. I'll take care of her."

"But you have a resort to run."

"Believe it or not, I have been known to multitask," he said, trying to ease his sister's panic.

"I'll believe *that* when I see it."

"Thanks for the call." He clipped his phone onto his belt and glanced at Nia. "My sister's afraid I can't take care of you."

Once uttered, the words took on a whole new meaning. It wasn't just about taking care of her by helping her process the break-in. The implication exposed the reality that Aiden, in fact, was not equipped to take care of a woman emotionally, even one he cared about deeply.

Nia frowned. "I feel bad taking you away from work. I'll head back to my apartment and check email from there."

"No." He stopped and looked into her sweet brown eyes. "You should stay at the resort in case the police need to speak with you."

She needed to stay close so he could protect her.

"Of course, but that won't take all afternoon," she said and kept walking.

As they approached Aiden's office, he tried coming up with other reasons to keep her here other than the obvious: he feared she might be in danger. What if she'd been in her office when the guy had broken in? Nia had been known to stay late at work, especially if there was an event planned for guests the next day and she wanted to make sure everything was in order.

"What's wrong?" she asked as he unlocked the door to his office.

"Nothing. Why?" He swung the door wide and held his breath. Nothing had been disturbed.

"You do this jaw-clench thing when you're stressing about something."

"Jaw clench, huh?"

"Yep. I know there's trouble when I see that."

"I don't like people breaking into my resort."

He motioned her to his computer, feeling exposed by the personal items lined up on his desk: a framed Seahawks ticket stub from the game he and his dad had attended years ago; a photo of Aiden, Bree, his sister Cassie and their mom, taken on the front porch of the farmhouse; and the Faith plaque Bree had given him when he'd returned from his tour of duty.

"'Faith is when you close your eyes and open your heart,'" Nia read. "That's lovely."

Aiden's eyes scanned the words every day, yet they never seemed to touch his heart. He placed the Peace figurine on his desk. "I'll get to this later."

"Thanks. Do I need a password?" Nia set her crutches against the bookshelves and adjusted herself in his chair.

He reached out to steady the chair, careful not to touch her. What was his problem? It wasn't as if a casual touch would hurt her.

Touching Nia in any way, shape or form would be way beyond casual.

She glanced at him. "You can change the password after I check my email."

"I trust you," he said, yet giving her the password would be awkward. He had no choice. "It's Yates627."

She typed it in and opened the email program. "So, what's a Yates?"

"Army buddy. Didn't make it back."

Her fingers froze as she typed in her email password. "Oh."

"Police are going to be looking for me," he said. "You okay in here?"

"Sure."

"Text me if you need anything."

Without thinking, he brushed his hand against her arm. He wasn't sure why he did it, but suspected it was his way of making a physical connection to the one person he'd told about Yates. He'd never before mentioned the guy's name, or the fact he'd died, to another human being, not even his own family.

Not until now.

He had to get out of here and fast, before she sensed the

shame coursing through him every time he thought about his friend.

"Aiden?" Nia said as he approached the door.

He turned to her.

"I am sorry about your friend. I'll say a prayer for your wounded heart."

With a nod, he left the office, a ball of emotion forming in his throat. *His wounded heart*, an apt description of the worst of his injuries he'd suffered while serving his country.

And Nia had been the only one to see it. The fact she was going to pray for him eased the tension in his chest, especially after everything she'd been through these past twenty-four hours. The woman was amazing.

Who knew, maybe her prayers would be heard and, through a lovely creature like Nia, God would find the mercy to help Aiden move through the darkness and into the light. Aiden may not be worth God's efforts, but Nia surely was.

He hesitated, wanting to go back and tell her not to waste her prayers on him, that she should save them for those who were more worthy. But then he'd have to explain why he didn't feel worthy of God's love, and that was not a conversation he could have with Nia, not today, not ever.

It took Nia a few minutes to digest Aiden's words. He'd lost a friend to battle, obviously a good friend since he used the man's name as his password, a daily reminder of their friendship. She wondered what the numbers 627 meant. Perhaps the man's birthday?

As her attention drifted from the doorway where Aiden had walked out with a defeated look on his face, she refocused on her immediate surroundings. The Faith plaque had such a calming effect on her when she read the words, yet she sensed they did nothing for Aiden's emotional pain.

Taking a deep breath, she folded her hands. "Dear Lord, please help Aiden find peace. He's such a good man and

suffers in silence, all alone. Please bless him with your love
to heal his wounded heart. Amen."

That was truly all she could do. Nia knew that you could
desperately want to help someone find emotional healing,
but unless they wanted it for themselves, it would never happen. The thought brought back memories of her mom crying
in her bedroom and Nia trying to console her. Mom wanted
out of a bad marriage to Walter but didn't have enough faith
in herself, or the Lord, to find her way to freedom. She would
agree to leave her abuser one day, yet two days later she'd
be in his arms, dancing in the living room. Walter could be
charming when he wanted to be.

A lot like Danny. Walter wasn't even Danny's biological
father, yet sometimes they seemed so much alike, perhaps
because Walter was Danny's male role model?

"Moving on," Nia whispered to redirect her thoughts
from the negative memories. There was no sense dwell-
ing on the past.

After she checked her email, she would head back to her
apartment, take Danny to the bank and get him the money
he needed to repay his boss. Done. He'd be free and clear
once again and on his way to settle things. Life would get
back to normal.

She glanced around Aiden's office, which only reminded
her how *not* normal life was at this very moment. Sure, she'd
wandered into his doorway at times, but she'd never breached
the threshold. She'd sensed Aiden liked his privacy.

She suddenly felt as if she shouldn't be here. She felt as
though she was violating his personal space.

"Check email and get moving," she ordered herself.

As she clicked open her emails, she scanned the subject
lines for anything urgent. She read an email from Scenic
Tours confirming a Seattle boat cruise scheduled for a group
coming in at the end of the week. The Metter reunion was
being hosted this weekend, and the family member who'd
booked the reservation wanted to line up special activities

for the attendees. She confirmed the boat tour and moved on to other emails.

She decided to check her spam folder in case something had inadvertently ended up there.

"How odd," she said, eyeing an email from Danny's account, Lionsfan20@wavemail.com. Since it was from two days ago, she figured he was letting her know he was coming to town. She clicked open the email, but all it contained was a website link. She'd have to let him know his email address had been hacked. And here she'd thought he was being polite by sending her an email notifying her of his visit.

A half hour later she was about to sign off, when Aiden stepped into the office. "The police are ready to talk to you whenever you're done."

"Okay, I'm finished." She grabbed her crutches before Aiden could lecture her yet again about using them. "Where are they?"

"Your office. Although I can have them interview you at another location if it's too upsetting to be there."

"Thanks, but I can handle it."

They headed down the hall.

"Any crises I should know about today?" she asked.

"Nothing I can't handle. Besides, you're officially off duty."

"Did the police figure out how someone got into my office?"

"Scott checked key-card activity, and someone entered at 3:00 a.m. and exited at three-thirty. We're thinking that might have been the intruder."

"Did you get him on security video?"

"We did, but the guy wore a hoodie and was looking down."

"Just one guy, huh? So it wasn't the two supposed federal agents?"

"No one's seen them since yesterday, and there's been no room activity. They'll probably send out a SAR team today to locate them."

She turned the corner to her office and hesitated in the doorway. Deputy Nate Walsh was going through her things. "Hi, Deputy Walsh."

"Please, call me Nate." Nate offered his hand and she shook it. "Glad you're okay."

"Thanks."

"If you wouldn't mind, could you go through your office and see if anything's missing? Even the smallest thing can help me figure out a motive for the break-in."

"Sure." She went into the office and Aiden followed. He was staying close. She wasn't sure why he was being so protective, especially since it was broad daylight and the deputy was with them.

As she fingered through the mess of papers on her desk, she puzzled over the motive for trashing her office.

"I can't really tell which files are missing without going through everything. But the passwords are safe. I keep them in my wallet."

"Forensics will swing by later today or tomorrow to dust for prints," Nate said. "So if you wouldn't mind working from another location—"

"She's actually taking a few days off," Aiden interrupted.

"Oh, she is, is she?" Nia said with a raised eyebrow.

"I think it's best," Aiden said.

"I could work from home."

"I'd rather you relax."

Aiden's phone vibrated and he stepped outside to take a call.

"He's very protective," Nate offered.

"Yeah, he's a good boss."

"Nia, can you think of any reason why someone would want to break into your office?"

"No. I live a pretty uneventful life and don't have any enemies—at least, I hope I don't."

"How about someone from your past?"

She snapped her attention to the handsome detective. "Why do you ask that?"

"Aiden said you don't talk much about your past, so I thought—"

"It's the past," she dismissed. "I left it behind years ago."

"I understand, but sometimes these things follow you."

She thought about her brother lying on her couch at home. "They do, don't they?" she whispered.

"Anything you want to share?" Nate asked.

"No, it's not pertinent to this situation." Besides, Danny would be gone and out of her life once she got him the money he needed. "Sorry I couldn't be more help in here," she said. "Guess I'll head home and follow my boss's orders to relax."

"Sounds good. I'll have Aiden let you know when Forensics is done in here."

"Thanks." She left her office and glanced down the hall toward the sound of Aiden's deep voice. She debated what to do. She didn't want to interrupt his call but didn't want to leave without saying goodbye. Leaning against the wall, she decided to wait a few minutes. His voice grew louder, but not because he was angry. He was headed in her direction.

"We've got open rooms until Thursday, when a big group checks in. The weekend is totally booked, but we can set up cots in the barn if necessary." He ran his hand through his thick blond hair and glanced at Nia.

She offered a smile. He put up a finger as if to say he needed a minute.

"I'm sure Quinn won't have a problem with it. How's the recovery effort going?…Sure…I can probably do that. I'll put my security manager in charge of the check-in process…Yep, will do, thanks."

Aiden nodded at Nia. "Apparently a group of hikers was trapped by the mud slide."

"Oh no."

"They're okay. But the SAR members who've been out

there since yesterday are beat, so the sheriff's office is requesting fresh SAR teams."

"Have they asked you to run field command?"

"Yes, but—" he glanced at her "—I should probably decline."

"Why would you do that?"

When he didn't immediately answer, she said, "Oh no, you are not turning your back on people who need you because you're worried about me. I won't have it."

"Nia—"

"Didn't I hear you say something about setting people up at the resort?" she said, changing the subject.

He motioned her down the hall. "Yes, there are about a dozen folks who can't get into their homes, so I'm offering them a place to stay until the weekend."

"I can help with that."

"Nia, I'd rather—"

"Please let me do this. I hate feeling useless."

He considered her request for a second. "Okay. After you take care of that, I'll have Scott drive you home."

"Not necessary. I'll drive myself."

"But your ankle—"

"It's my left ankle. Shouldn't be a problem. You go help with the rescue."

He hesitated at the exit door. "Are you sure? I have no problem staying back."

"Well, I do, so get moving, boss."

With a nod, he pushed open the door, and she watched him march to his truck. Aiden was at his best when he was on a search-and-rescue mission. He seemed more himself, more confident and natural with everyone he came into contact with. It seemed as if helping others made him feel whole.

She was so glad she'd convinced him to go.

An hour later Nia finished making arrangements for the displaced residents but then got caught up in other work-related issues and spent the rest of the afternoon at the resort. She always did have a hard time setting her boundaries.

She struggled to set aside her disappointment about the broken Peace figurine. It wasn't valuable in a monetary way but had sentimental meaning that went beyond dollars and cents. It was the figurine she'd bought when she'd left the darkness behind and started her new life, an independent life focused on hope, faith and belief in herself. She appreciated that Aiden had offered to fix it for her.

At four o'clock she decided to end her workday and get to the bank to make the withdrawal for her brother. She didn't have time to stop by and pick him up.

She'd been saving money for a special, exotic vacation of some kind, but with her work ethic and hours, it wasn't likely she'd take one anytime soon. Giving her brother the money seemed like the right thing to do. She still had a couple thousand in her account, so parting with the funds wasn't a huge crisis.

By the time she arrived home at five-thirty, she found Danny stretched out on the couch, asleep.

"Hey, lazy boy, wake up." She poked him in the stomach.

He awoke suddenly and grabbed her wrist, squeezing it tight.

"Danny, you're hurting me," she said.

His eyes finally focused and his fingers sprang free of her hand. "Sorry, sorry. What time is it?"

"Five-thirty," she said, a little anxious about his grip on her wrist. "What'd you do, sleep all day?"

"No, I went for a run, took a shower and then took a nap." He grinned.

"Great, well, I swung by the bank and got your loan."

"My loan?"

She pulled the envelope out of her purse and dropped it in his lap. "You're paying me back this time, little brother."

"Of course, of course I am."

But they both knew he wouldn't.

She flopped down on a chair across the room. "Want to get dinner? I'm starving."

"Sure," he said, but seemed more interested in counting the cash.

"How about I order Mexican or Chinese food?"

"Sounds good," he said.

She pulled out her cell phone. "Which?"

"Huh?" He glanced at her.

"Mexican or Chinese?"

"Mexican's great. I'll pick it up."

Nia called in the order. A few minutes later Danny left to pick up the food, saying he wanted to stop by the grocery store for soda. She suspected he'd come home with a six-pack of beer. Whatever. It was one dinner, and he'd be gone, off to settle his business with his sketchy employer. How did he always end up working with questionable people? Hadn't he learned anything from his arrest as a teenager? Jail wasn't a place he should aspire to call home.

Danny needed to let go of his past the way Nia had and move on, start a new life with a legitimate job. In the meantime, she could at least help him out of this tight spot.

An hour later when Danny hadn't returned, Nia grew worried. She called him but got his voice mail. Maybe the order had been messed up and he was on his way home but couldn't answer her call while driving. She hoped so. She hoped he hadn't stopped for a beer at the local pub and made new friends he found more interesting than his sister.

She went to the fridge and grabbed an apple. If he didn't get home soon she'd call the restaurant to see if the order had been picked up. Her cell phone rang from her purse in the bedroom.

"There you are," she said. She went into her room and dug the phone out of her purse sitting on the bed. It was a blocked number. *Figures.*

"Danny, where are you?" she said, assuming it was him.

"So, your brother's still in town?" Aiden said.

"Aiden, hi. What's with the blocked number?"

"New phone."

"How'd the mission go?"

"Quite well, thanks. We rescued the stranded hikers, so I'm headed back and thought I'd check in."

"That's great. No serious injuries?"

"No, ma'am, although some pretty harrowing stories are being told by the survivors. You were expecting your brother to call?"

"He went to pick up dinner and he's late. No big deal."

"Sure it is. I can hear the hunger in your voice."

"Very funny."

The sound of the squeaking front door echoed across the apartment. She wandered toward the living room. "Problem solved. He's—"

She froze at the sight of a stranger standing in her living room, staring at her. He was tall, in his midforties and looked as if he worked construction.

"What are you doing in my apartment?" Nia said.

"Nia, what's going on?" Aiden asked.

"I'm looking for Danny Sharpe," the intruder said.

"He's not here," she said, lowering the phone but not ending the call.

Instinct told her to remain calm.

"Is that him on the phone? Is that Danny?" the man asked.

She nodded, anticipating his next move. As expected, he stuck out his hand and she handed him the phone, edging backward, away from him. She hoped Aiden would figure out what to do next.

The stranger held the phone to his ear. "I'm here at your sister's place. If you ever want to see her again, be here in twenty minutes."

# FIVE

Aiden didn't respond at first, stunned by what was happening.

"Did you hear me?" the voice said.

"Yes."

Then nothing. Dead silence.

Struggling to get control of his panic, Aiden pressed a button on his phone and directed the intelligence personal assistant to call 911.

"Nine-one-one, what's your emergency?"

"My name is Aiden McBride. Someone broke into my friend's apartment and is threatening her life. You need to send a squad car over there, ASAP."

"What's the address, sir?"

He gave the operator Nia's full name and address. "It's apartment two, ground floor."

"And you think she's being threatened because...?"

"The man said if I ever wanted to see her again I'd better show up in the next twenty minutes. I don't think I can get there in twenty minutes. I'm out on Route 2 headed back from the Rockland mud slide."

"Okay, sir, I understand. I'll send a car right away. Do you have her phone number? I'd like to call her."

Aiden gave Dispatch her number, then decided to call Nate.

"Deputy Walsh," he answered.

"Nate, it's Aiden. Where are you?"

"In town picking up groceries. Why?"

"How fast can you get to Nia's apartment? Someone broke in, he's there now and—"

"I'm on my way."

"Thanks."

Aiden pressed the earpiece to end the call with one hand, his other hand gripping the steering wheel with deadly force.

A man had broken into Nia's place and Aiden wasn't there to protect her. Guilt arced through his chest.

Slamming his palm against the steering wheel, he hit the accelerator but caught himself and eased up on the pedal. He wouldn't get there quicker if he was pulled over for speeding.

Shoving aside his dread, he replayed the phone call in his mind. The guy thought Aiden was her brother, which meant Aiden's instincts had been right on: Danny was bad news and he'd brought it with him to Echo Mountain.

The next twenty-plus minutes were a blur as Aiden focused on getting to Nia. When he finally pulled up in front of her apartment, he spotted Nate's unmarked police car parked out front. Aiden rushed into the building and pounded on Nia's door.

A few seconds later, Nate swung it open. "She's okay," he said, motioning Aiden into the hallway.

Why couldn't Aiden go inside? Had she been assaulted? Was her face bruised? Nate probably knew Aiden might lose it if that was the case.

"What aren't you telling me?" Aiden said. "Why can't I see her?"

"She's fine, and I'll tell you everything if you'd dial it down a notch."

Aiden glared at his friend and took a breath, hissing through his teeth.

"I got here about the same time as Officer Carrington and Chief Washburn," Nate started.

"The chief came?"

"He was close and heard the call. We came up with a

plan. I knocked, pretending to be a friend, while Carrington broke in through Nia's bedroom window. My goal was to get her out of there safely. When she cracked open the door, I shoved it open and grabbed her as Carrington charged the perp from the bedroom. He tackled the guy and the chief cuffed him while I shielded Nia from the scene. They took the man to lockup and wanted me to stay with Nia, ask her a few questions if she's up to it."

"And is she?"

"I can't tell. One minute she's all fired up, and the next she seems defeated, like she's given up. She'd just made tea, which seemed to relax her, when you showed up." Nate frowned at Aiden. "She practically jumped out of her skin when you banged on the door. She's fragile, Aiden. I suggest a softer tone than usual."

"You mean, don't be my typical charming self?" Aiden said sarcastically.

"I don't mean to tell you how to act with your girl—"

"She's not my girl. She's the resort concierge." The moment he said the words he felt ashamed.

Nate studied him. "Okay, well, your resort concierge is more than a bit shaken up right now. Please keep that in mind when you talk to her, okay?"

Aiden nodded, hating that his friend had to coach him on how to act with Nia.

"Do you want some privacy?" Nate asked.

"No," Aiden said, almost too anxious. "Finish your questioning."

Aiden was uncomfortable at the thought of being alone with Nia. Why? Did he fear he'd take her in his arms and hold on until he knew she was okay? Even if that meant holding her all night long?

With a nod, Nate pushed open the door.

Aiden entered an empty living room. "Where is she?"

"I don't know, perhaps the bathroom? She said she needed a cool washcloth for her headache."

"Please tell me he didn't hit her," Aiden said between clenched teeth.

"No, she said he didn't touch her. I think it's all the stress she's been under since the fall yesterday."

With a nod, Aiden went into the kitchen to pour a cup of tea. Maybe it would relax him and ease the tension humming across his nerve endings.

No, the only thing that would ease his anxiety was seeing Nia's smiling face.

"Who was at the door?" Nia said to Nate in the other room.

Aiden stepped out of the kitchen and she glanced at him with such relief in her eyes. The way he'd pounded on the door probably made her think her attacker's partner had shown up.

"Aiden," she gasped, limping across the room. She hugged him, pressing her cheek against his chest.

He stopped himself from yet another lecture about using the crutches and stroked her hair. "Shh, everything's okay now."

"I'm so glad I was talking to you when it happened. I knew you'd figure out how to save me."

"Yeah, a big help from ten miles away."

"Hey—" she leaned back and looked up at him "—the police came because of you. If they hadn't shown up when they did…" Her voice cracked.

Aiden pulled her against his chest. "They came. You're all right."

A few seconds passed and he gently led her to the dining room table.

"Did you have more questions?" he asked Nate.

"Sure, if she's up to it."

"I am," Nia said, sitting down.

Nate and Aiden joined her at the table. Aiden resisted the urge to reach out and hold her hand. While hugging her, the reality of how close he'd come to losing Nia tore him apart inside.

"Did the man give you any clue why he was here?" Nate asked.

"He was looking for my brother, Danny."

"Why did he think Danny would be here?"

"Danny randomly showed up last night. I haven't seen him in—" she paused "—probably three years. We talk, of course," she added, as if she feared she looked like a bad sister.

Aiden knew if anyone had failed as a sibling, it was her brother.

"And the man who broke in threatened your life?" Nate asked.

She nodded and glanced at Aiden.

"He said if I ever wanted to see her again, I'd better get here in twenty," Aiden said. "He thought I was Danny."

"And you sensed this threat was genuine?" Nate asked Aiden.

"Yes" was all Aiden could get out as emotion tangled his vocal cords. Anger that he hadn't been here to protect her; fear that he could have lost her.

Lost her? *She's not yours to lose, McBride.*

"Where's your brother now?" Nate asked.

"I don't know," Nia said. "He went to pick up dinner over an hour ago and never returned."

"Maybe that's a good thing," Aiden muttered.

"Do you have any idea why the intruder was looking for him?"

"Won't the chief ask him that during interrogation?" Aiden said.

"I got a text that the guy already lawyered up." Nate glanced at Nia. "Any idea what he was after?"

"It probably has something to do with the two thousand dollars Danny gambled away. It wasn't his money to lose."

"Whose money was it?" Nate asked.

"I'm not sure. Danny was collecting money for someone, probably a loan shark. But it doesn't matter since I gave Danny the money and he was going to pay back his boss."

"You gave him the money?" Aiden asked.

"Why do you say it like that? What was I supposed to do?" she said, her tone rising. "He's my brother and he needed my help."

Aiden suspected he'd hit a sore spot and wondered if deep down she questioned her own decision to bail Danny out. Aiden suspected it wasn't the first time.

"We'd better figure out a way to keep you safe until we clear this up," Nate said.

"She'll stay at the resort," Aiden said.

"Wait—slow down," Nia protested.

"It's the best course of action."

"Nate, can you give us a few minutes alone?"

"Sure."

Great, Aiden was probably in for a lecture on how she didn't like being told what to do. He'd listen, acknowledge her feelings and then convince her that staying at the resort—or better yet, at Bree's cottage with her newly installed, high-tech security system—was the best decision.

"I'll be outside if you need me," Nate said and left the apartment.

Nia turned to Aiden.

"Go ahead. Let me have it," Aiden said.

"I'm sorry."

"Wait—what? You're sorry for what?"

"I can't give you two weeks' notice."

"What are you talking about?"

"I'm resigning, effective immediately."

Aiden's devastated expression cut Nia to the quick. But this was the best decision, the only way to keep Aiden and her friends at Echo Mountain Resort safe.

"I guess I should have made that sound more like a suggestion than an order," Aiden said.

"What?"

"You've finally had enough of my demanding nature."

"No, Aiden—"

"It's fine." Aiden got up and paced to the window. "Bree's been on my case about my tone. You're done. I get it."

"That's not it," Nia said.

He turned to her, and her heart broke. He looked as if he'd just lost his best friend, not one of his best employees.

"I need to leave town to keep everyone safe," she said.

"What are you talking about?"

She shook her head and glanced at the taupe carpeting. "I should have known something like this would happen."

"Something like what?" He came back to the table and sat down. "You did nothing wrong."

"Maybe not, but my past has caught up to me, so I need to move on."

"You're running away from this?" He leaned back in his chair with an incredulous frown.

"I wouldn't call it running as much as protecting my friends."

"I'd call it running, and that surprises me. I mean, you're such a determined, strong person, yet you're letting your brother's mistakes drive you away from your home? You do consider Echo Mountain your home, right?"

"You know I do."

"Then why let your brother take it away from you?"

"You make it sound like he planned this. He didn't plan to put me in danger."

"I'm missing something here. What?" He leaned forward and stared earnestly into her eyes.

"I'm not sure what you want me to say, Aiden."

"You're a tough woman, so why are you cowering from the consequences of your brother's bad decisions?"

"I'm a realist, not a coward."

"I didn't say you were a coward, but you're surrendering awfully quickly and sacrificing things you care about, especially your friends and your church community."

*And you,* she thought.

She blinked and broke eye contact. "It can't be helped."

"Because?"

She didn't answer. If only she'd successfully protected Danny from their stepfather growing up, things would be different. Danny would be different.

"You need to cut ties with your brother and stop enabling him by giving him money," Aiden said.

"Aiden," she hushed. "He's my brother."

"He's a grown man and should be taking care of himself."

"If he needs my help I have to be there for him, no matter what."

"He's pulling you down, Nia. He'll continue to drag you into his mess until you hit the stop button. He's not your responsibility."

"He's my little brother."

"Who's involved in some sketchy stuff."

"Well, maybe if I'd been there for him…"

The shame drifting off her body was almost palpable. There, she'd said it. Aiden had forced it out of her.

"Nia, you can't feel responsible for your brother's decisions as an adult."

"You don't know what it was like in our house. And I left him behind so I could go to college. Selfish girl." She stood and started for the kitchen, needing to get away from Aiden and the truth.

Aiden touched her shoulder. "Hey, hey, where are you going?"

"Kitchen. For a snack."

"Sit down. I'll get it."

She didn't look at him. She couldn't. Now that he knew the truth, she felt even more ashamed.

Collapsing on the chair, she wished that Nate would come

back so they could stop talking about this. She didn't enjoy reliving the past, thinking about what she should have done for her brother. Whom she could have told.

In retrospect, the list was lengthy. She could have exposed Walter's cruelty, told any one of her high school teachers, her pastor, her mom's best friend, someone. Instead, she'd kept the truth of Walter's abuse a secret because her mother begged her to, and as long as Nia lived at home, she felt she could protect Danny from the abuse.

Then she'd decided she wanted a life for herself, a career, which meant she had to abandon him. He'd never made her feel guilty about leaving and even told her how proud he was that she'd "gotten out."

But she should have known that growing up in a violent atmosphere would have residual effects. Each week at church she'd include Danny in her prayers and ask for forgiveness for being selfish.

Eventually she'd even reached the point of self-forgiveness.

Then Danny showed up, and she felt horrible all over again.

"How about cheese and crackers?" Aiden said from the kitchen.

"Sounds good."

A few minutes later, Aiden rejoined her at the table with a plate of sliced cheese and a box of crackers. "You need more tea?"

"No, I'm okay."

"I guess it all makes sense now."

"What?" she said, reaching for a piece of cheese.

"Why you're so good at taking care of everyone else. You took care of your brother and probably your mom, too, right?"

She nodded.

A soft knock echoed across the room. "Guess Nate's back," Aiden said and pointedly looked at Nia. "We're not done with this conversation."

She nodded but knew she couldn't let him change her mind about leaving town. She cared too much about the people here. About Aiden.

He opened the door. "What's that look?" Aiden asked Nate.

"Maybe it's nothing, but a suspicious vehicle cruised by the apartment building awfully slow a minute ago. Nia, I suggest you pack a bag and move out for a couple of days until we get this squared away."

Aiden nodded at her. "It's settled. You'll move into Bree's place, at least temporarily."

She opened her mouth to speak, but he cut her off.

"I need to protect you, Nia. Please let me do that."

It was his tone that made Nia swallow her protest. She'd never heard him speak like that before, so gentle and almost pleading. She felt the pain in his words and couldn't stand that she'd caused it.

"Okay, I'll pack my things."

An hour later, Nia was settled at Bree's kitchen table, icing her ankle and nibbling the burrito she'd ordered and Danny had never picked up. Aiden suggested they swing by the restaurant on the way to the resort. The food was still there. Danny was nowhere to be found.

Nia wasn't all that hungry but knew she should eat something. The past twenty-four hours had sapped her energy and strung her nerves as tight as a tennis racket. She was upset with her brother but also worried about him. She couldn't believe he'd taken her money and disappeared without even saying goodbye or warning her that a man might come looking for him.

As she continued to puzzle over his behavior, Bree came into the kitchen, followed by her golden retriever, Fiona. "How's the ankle?"

"Better, actually. It wasn't that serious to begin with."

"Want some cookies?"

"Sure, okay."

Bree raised an eyebrow. "Or maybe you're tired. That's okay, too."

"I feel bad putting you out."

"Are you kidding? I love having company. I've got a second bedroom that's hardly ever used." Bree opened the refrigerator. "Milk?"

"Sure." Nia glanced down the hall at the front door.

Bree turned around and eyed Nia. "I'm sure he'll be back."

"What?" Nia looked at Bree. "Who?"

"My brother."

"No, I wasn't…"

"It's okay. I won't tell anyone." Bree smiled.

"Tell anyone…?"

"That you're his new project."

"What do you mean?"

"When someone's in trouble he's quick to jump to the rescue."

"Yeah, I guess you're right." Nia had certainly seen enough of Aiden's helpful side, with family, friends and sometimes even guests.

"Unless you want to be more than just his project?" Bree winked.

"No, of course not. He's my boss."

"Uh-huh."

"Don't start something here, Bree. I'm not going to be around that long anyway," Nia said.

"What are you talking about?"

Suddenly Fiona rushed out of the kitchen, barking frantically in the living room.

"Fiona, no!" Bree called out, but the dog didn't stop. "Sometimes she goes crazy when deer roam the property. But she usually stops when I give the command."

With a concerned frown, Bree headed for the living room

and Nia followed. They went to the window where Fiona was barking and pounding on the glass with her paws.

Nia looked outside…

And saw Aiden in a fistfight with a stranger.

# SIX

"Aiden!" Nia spun around and started for the door.

"Nia, stop." Bree darted in front of her. "We'll call for help."

"But—"

"Aiden wouldn't want you to put yourself in danger. You know that."

Nia nodded and turned back to the window as Bree made the call. "Scott, you need to get over here. Aiden is fighting with some guy out front…Okay, I will." She turned to Nia. "I'm calling 911."

Nia squinted to see out the window, but Aiden and his attacker were out of sight. "Where'd they go?" She went to another window but couldn't see past the darkness.

"This is Bree McBride at Echo Mountain Resort. I'd like to report an assault taking place outside my cottage," Bree said into the phone.

"I can't see them. Bree, they're gone," Nia said. She spotted the security truck racing toward the cottage, the orange light flashing on the roof.

Bree peered out the window. "Resort security is on the way," she said to the 911 operator.

Someone pounded on the front door and both women shrieked.

"Breanna, open the door!" Aiden called from the other side.

Nia beat Bree to the door and whipped it open. She gasped at the sight of his bloody lip and the scratches on his face. He clutched his arm against his stomach as if it was injured.

"Your arm?" Nia said.

"Arm's okay. Think I cracked a rib."

"Is he gone?" Bree said.

"Yeah, he took off around the house and I heard his car peel out. I tried to detain him but failed."

He thought he'd failed? Nia's heart pounded against her chest.

Bree pulled him into the house. "Nia, take him back to the kitchen for first aid. I'll wait here for Scott."

Nia hesitated, knowing this was her fault, all her fault.

"Nia?" Bree prompted.

Tears welled in her eyes as she looked at Aiden. "I'm sorry," she said.

"What are you…? Oh no, Nia, don't do that." He pulled her against his chest. "We don't know that this is related to your brother's situation."

Nia pushed away. "Of course it is. Now do you understand why I have to leave?"

Nia headed for the kitchen. The least she could do before she left town was tend to his wounds, apply ice and make him something warm to drink. She grabbed a kitchen towel and ran it under warm water.

"Go ahead and sit at the table," she said.

"Nia—"

"Please, Aiden."

She heard him pull out the chair behind her. She squeezed moisture from the towel and went to him, pressing the cloth to his upper right cheek. He winced slightly and she jerked her hand back.

"Go ahead. It doesn't hurt," he said, his eyes intent on her.

"You winced."

"I'm not used to people touching me." He hesitated. "It's fine."

She pressed the warm cloth against a cut on his cheekbone.

"Where are your crutches?" he asked.

She pointed across the kitchen where they leaned against the counter. "What happened out there?"

"I saw some guy peeking into Bree's living room window."

"You saw him from the resort? That's awfully far away."

"I was headed over to check on you."

"Oh, so this really *is* my fault."

"No, it isn't." He looked at her with intense blue eyes. "I don't want to ever hear you say that again. Okay?"

Nia sighed. "Do you know what he wanted?"

"He wasn't a chatty type of guy. When I asked him what he was doing he took a swing at me."

"So he's probably another man looking for my brother. All over two grand?"

Aiden shot her a skeptical look.

"You're thinking there's more to this than a missing two thousand dollars, aren't you?" Nia said.

"Seems like a lot of trouble for a couple of grand, if this guy is even one of the guys looking for your brother."

"As opposed to some random Peeping Tom," Nia retorted.

"We shouldn't assume anything." He winced again and she pulled away.

"Maybe you should." She motioned to the cloth. "I hate that I'm hurting you."

"You're not."

His gaze caught hers and she couldn't look away. This man had been through enough pain, enough trauma in his life. He didn't need more piled on because of her.

Scott and Bree entered the kitchen. "Police are on the way," Scott said. "How bad were you hurt?"

"Not bad," Aiden said.

Scott sat across the table from him. "Did you recognize the guy?"

"No, but I can give police a decent description."

"We may not need it if resort security cameras got a clear shot of him."

Nia stood.

"Nia?" Aiden questioned.

"I need to pack my things. I'll call a car service and have them take me to the airport tonight."

"Wait—where are you going?" Bree asked.

"It's probably best if you don't know." Nia headed into the hallway, frustration tearing her apart.

"Nia, hang on," Aiden said. He caught up to her and handed her the crutches. "Sit with me for a second?"

It was a soft-spoken request, so unlike his usual tone. He must be hurting from the fight.

"Sure."

They went into the living room and sat on the sofa.

"I realize you think leaving is the best for everyone," he said.

"It is."

"I disagree. It's not the best for you, is it?" Aiden questioned, pinning her with those incredible blue eyes.

She glanced at her fingers in her lap. "What's best for me doesn't matter."

"How can you say that?"

"Aiden—"

"Hear me out. You've got friends here, good friends, and a great job, right?"

"Yes, but I can't put those friends in danger. After what happened tonight—"

"That was my fault. I went after the guy instead of calling Security. My choice. Now I need you to reconsider yours. You can skip town, but know this—the past will keep following you."

"What if that man had broken into Bree's house?"

"Trust me, Bree knows how to handle herself, and Scott would have been here within seconds of the alarm going off."

"Aiden, I have to protect them."

Silence filled the room. Had she convinced him of her goal?

"Nia, remember all those days I was working at minimum power because I wasn't sleeping?"

She glanced down. She did but never would have brought it up.

"You know what I'm talking about," he said. "I could have lost my job as manager of the resort. I could have messed up my future, big-time, but you propped me up and kept things running. I'd like to return the favor and help you through this."

"That's sweet. It really is."

"But?"

"It's my battle to fight."

"And you're going to fight it by running away?"

"It's the best strategy."

"Not from where I'm sitting." He took her hand, and her breath caught in her throat. "You've been strong for me. Now be strong for yourself. Don't run. Stand firm and fight, and we'll be right there with you. Me and my sister, and all your friends from the resort and church."

"No, if someone got hurt…" She hesitated. "If you were hurt…" she croaked.

"I'm tough and I know you are, too. Don't let the past steal one more minute of your future, okay?"

With a nod, she realized she'd never thought of it that way.

When Aiden awoke on Bree's sofa the next morning, his sister was standing over him with a wry smile on her face.

"What?" he said.

"Good morning to you, too. Here's your coffee." She handed him a mug.

He sat up a little too fast and clenched his jaw against the pain of sore ribs.

"Yeah, you're really tough," Bree said.

He snapped his attention to her.

"I overheard some of your lecture to Nia last night," Bree admitted.

He grabbed the mug, took a sip and moaned, closing his eyes. His sister had a way with coffee.

"It wasn't a lecture," he said.

"Okay, big brother."

He glanced toward the stairs, worried. "She didn't leave, did she?"

"Nope. Still in her room. Asleep, I hope. She needs the rest after everything she's been through."

"Thanks again for letting her stay with you."

"Of course. She's a welcome addition to my family."

Aiden narrowed his eyes.

"What? It gets lonely with just me and Fiona," Bree said. "And I have a feeling my future husband is going to want something bigger in which to raise our children."

"Children? Whoa, you're not even married yet. We are talking about Scott, right?" he teased.

Giggling, she gave him a playful smack on the head. "You're smarter than you look." She turned and started for the kitchen. "I made Swedish pancakes for breakfast, with jam and whipped butter."

Aiden leaned back and sipped his coffee, smiling about his sister's giggle. It had been a long time since he'd heard that sound, the sound of joy. He was glad she'd found it again, especially with a solid guy like Scott.

"You coming?" Her voice carried down the hall.

He stood and bit back a groan when he spotted Nia standing in the hall. She studied him with a worried look in her eyes.

"I'm glad you're still here," he said.

"You made a compelling argument."

He motioned them toward the kitchen. "Dad always

thought I'd make a great lawyer." He felt a pang of loss at the mention of his father.

"You're sore from fighting with that guy last night, aren't you?" she pressed.

"Nah, it's sleeping on Bree's uncomfortable sofa."

"Yeah, right," Nia said sarcastically as they entered the kitchen.

"What? Ask Scott. He'll confirm it."

"Confirm what?" Bree was setting the table.

"That your sofa was not designed to be slept on," Aiden said.

"Aren't you picky? Fiona loves the sofa, don't you, puppy dog?"

Fiona's ears perked up.

"She just wants a taste of your pancakes." Aiden shifted into a chair at the table. "I should call Nate and see if they found anything on that guy from last night."

"How about we eat first?" Bree said, shooting him a look.

Aiden glanced at Nia, who nibbled her lower lip. The mention of last night's intruder must have upset her.

Bree placed the dish of pancakes in the center of the table, along with small bowls of butter and jam.

"Man, I'm hungry." Aiden reached out with his fork.

Bree cleared her throat. Aiden froze and glanced at Nia, who reached for his hand. He put down the utensil and gave Nia his hand. Then Bree reached out for his other hand. Why did he suddenly feel ambushed? Nia cleared her throat and said the prayer.

"God is Great, God is Good. Let us thank Him for our food. By His hands we all are fed. Give us Lord our Daily Bread. Amen."

"Amen," Bree and Aiden said.

It wasn't as if he hadn't said the prayer before, especially at a family meal, but for some reason it felt different when Nia said it. It felt more personal.

Bree served them each a generous helping of pancakes

and offered Nia the fruit bowl. "What's on the agenda today?"

"I'll know that when I get to the office," Aiden said.

"Who said I was asking you?" Bree winked, then glanced at Nia.

Aiden jumped in. "She's relaxing today."

"Oh, I am, am I?" Nia said.

Aiden glanced at his sister. "Did I say that wrong? I said that wrong, didn't I?"

Bree bit back a smile.

"Let me try again." Aiden turned to Nia. "Would you mind staying at Bree's and relaxing today? You can make yourself available to staff by phone, but maybe not do any running around the resort like a crazy person?"

"Is that what I look like at work?" Nia glanced at Bree.

"No, that's not what I meant," Aiden said.

"Aren't you the one who said I shouldn't hide from this?"

"I'm not talking about hiding. I want…" He hesitated. "I'd feel better if you took another day for yourself to relax and recover from the last thirty-six hours."

"A nice thought, but I have to check on plans for the Metter reunion tomorrow, plus follow up on transportation and vouchers for the Waterfront Festival this weekend. Oh, and I need to pick a film for movie night."

"It's a good thing you didn't skip town," Bree said. "People depend on you."

Yeah, like Aiden. If he wanted to keep Nia around, he had to make her feel safe and respected.

"I'll assign someone to watch the cottage today while you're taking it easy," he said, cutting into his pancakes. "That is, if you decide to take it easy."

"Fine, I'll stay here today. But no one needs to babysit me."

"All the same—" His ringing phone cut off his response. He snapped it off his belt. "McBride."

"Hello, sir, it's Tripp at the front desk. The electrician is here to rewire the community room and says he has to cut power to the south end of the building."

"How many rooms are occupied in that wing?"

"About ten, sir. Also, someone from the chamber of commerce called about their meeting for thirty members at ten, but I don't have anything on the schedule, and—"

"I'll be right there."

"Yes, sir."

Aiden shoved a forkful of pancakes into his mouth and stood.

"What's wrong?" Nia asked.

He shook his head, trying to enjoy his one bite of breakfast.

"Is it work?" Nia pressed.

Aiden nodded.

"Bree, do you have any paper plates?" Nia asked.

"Sure." Bree got up and went to the pantry.

Aiden started to leave, but Nia blocked him. "Hang on. You can't start your day on an empty stomach."

Nia took a paper plate from Bree, slid Aiden's pancakes onto it, along with a spoonful of berries. Anticipating Nia's plan, Bree rifled through her drawers for a plastic fork.

"You can eat on the way." Nia walked him to the front door.

"I haven't even showered yet," he said, frustrated.

"What was the call about?"

"Electrician wants to shut down power to the south end of the resort, and someone from the chamber expects a room for thirty people to be set up by ten."

"I thought they'd canceled this month's meeting."

"Apparently so did Tripp."

"I'll take care of the chamber thing. You meet with the electrician, give him instructions and sneak out for a quick shower."

"Sounds like I'm going to have to move guests out of the south wing."

"Maybe not. Let me work on that."

He hesitated at the door. "Hang on. You were supposed to relax."

"It's fine. This will keep me from going stir-crazy."

"Are you sure?"

"Absolutely."

"At least ice the ankle."

"Will do."

"Okay, I'll touch base later." Aiden hesitated, and for a second he had the urge to go in for a hug but wasn't sure why. She must have read it in his eyes because she awkwardly leaned into him, then stepped back.

"Have a good day," she said.

"Thanks."

Aiden crossed the threshold onto the front porch and felt an odd sense of something, a connection he wasn't used to, and one he never thought he'd feel.

"Focus," he said to himself as he crossed the property to the main lodge, eating pancakes along the way. He needed to get the work-related issues taken care of, then contact police to see if they'd made progress with the man who'd threatened Nia last night, or if they'd located the Peeping Tom.

Nia might have sent him away with a plate of pancakes so he wouldn't go hungry, but he felt their roles were shifting. Instead of Nia always taking care of Aiden, Aiden was in a position to be strong and protect Nia.

He wished he had more confidence in his ability to keep her safe.

By early afternoon Aiden sensed it was going to be one of those up-for-grabs days, the kind when if something could go wrong it most certainly would. This type of day would have gone much smoother if Nia were on duty, working from her office. Aiden called her twice with questions but resisted asking her to come to the office. It was important that she take it easy and ice her ankle.

Aiden had wanted to check in on her at the cottage—because only face-to-face contact would truly ease his concern—but there'd been no time.

She'd texted him that she was able to find space for the chamber meeting. A few hours later, as Aiden passed by the room, he noticed she'd ordered a nice spread of fruit and scones through the food service department. She'd also checked in with the guests who would be without power that morning and offered them another room in a different part of the complex plus a complimentary meal and 30 percent off a tour of their choice. Rather than move, the guests said they'd prefer to stay in their rooms and didn't mind the minor inconvenience. Most had plans to be off resort grounds anyway.

The electrician's project took longer than anticipated, yet afternoon tea went off without a hitch, which surprised Aiden since everything else seemed to be destined for disaster.

It was fast closing in on suppertime, and he was finally about to head over to the cottage, when his phone rang.

"McBride," he answered.

"Aiden, it's Nate."

"You've got something?"

"A few things, yes."

Aiden instinctively sat down behind his desk. "Go on."

"The two men who were looking for you were, in fact, undercover federal agents."

"Why undercover? And what did they want with me?"

"Not sure yet. The Bureau is sending another team to explain things in person. They're worried the original agents' covers were blown, and something happened to them in the mountains. It's been forty-eight hours since they checked in."

"Are you going to—"

"It's done. A search-and-rescue text is going out shortly. And Aiden, there's something else."

Aiden rubbed his forehead with his fingertips. "What?"

"The man who broke into Nia's apartment last night made bail."

Aiden stood abruptly. "How's that possible?"

"The man's name is Gus Chambers, works for an import/ export business back in Detroit. He said her door was unlocked and he didn't physically harm her, so his lawyer was able to secure bail."

"He threatened her life," Aiden protested.

"He claims he was threatening the brother because of the money he stole from Gus's boss, not two grand, but two hundred thousand dollars."

"Oh man."

"And their only connection to Danny is Nia. His lawyer guaranteed us Gus wouldn't go anywhere near her again," Nate said.

"And you believed him?"

"He'd be stupid to approach her."

"Criminals aren't rocket scientists," Aiden said.

"Here's the good news. I circulated a video shot we got from security cameras. The Peeping Tom was ID'd as a criminal suspected of a string of burglaries in King County. Authorities were closing in on him, so they suspect he moved his operation up to Echo County."

"So that had nothing to do with the brother's situation?"

"Doesn't look like it. We've got a BOLO out on him. We'll be on the lookout."

"Okay, thanks."

"Oh, and Aiden, the two agents coming to town want to meet with you."

"About what?"

"They wouldn't say over the phone. We'll have to wait until tomorrow."

The pounding of footsteps echoed down the hall. Scott popped his head into Aiden's office, out of breath. "The cottage. The alarm went off."

# SEVEN

Aiden would have sprinted across the property, but Scott grabbed his arm and pulled him toward the security truck.

"Is Bree home?" Aiden said.

"Not yet."

They hopped into the truck and sped across the parking lot to the two-bedroom cottage.

Maybe Nia forgot to set it and went outside for fresh air, or maybe Fiona caught a whiff of a rabbit and took off with Nia in hot pursuit.

It had to be one of these things, because the alternative...

As they closed in on the house, Aiden fought back the possibilities that were terrorizing his mind.

"The guy who threatened her last night was released on bail," he said.

"What? After threatening her life?" Scott said.

Aiden shook his head. Gripped the dashboard.

Scott pulled up to the cottage. Aiden flung open his door and raced up the stairs.

"I'll check around back!" Scott said.

Aiden pounded on the door. "Nia!"

Fiona barked in response.He tried the door, but it was locked. He pulled out the master key and let himself inside.

"Nia!" he called out.

Silence.

Aiden rushed into the kitchen holding his breath for fear he'd find her unconscious on the floor.

The kitchen was empty.

Frantic, he rushed upstairs, Fiona hot on his heels, and checked both bedrooms, also empty. He went through closets; checked the two bathrooms. It was as if she'd disappeared.

As he rushed back into the guest room, he noticed her suitcase on the luggage rack, and on the nightstand beside the bed sat Nia's Bible.

She trusted in the Lord for love and compassion, and she trusted Aiden to protect her.

His heart pounded against his chest. What had happened to her?

"Aiden!" Scott called from the bottom of the stairs. "Her car's gone!"

Which meant what? That she and an intruder had fled in her car? That would be easy to find.

Aiden rushed down the stairs. "I'll call Nate."

"Maybe she went to the store."

"No, she wouldn't do that." Aiden called his friend and gave Nate the make, model and plate number of Nia's car.

"You sure she's not running errands?" Nate asked.

"No, she promised to stay at the cottage."

"Have you called her?"

"Not yet."

"Call her. See if you can track her down. I can't do anything official, but I can certainly spread the word."

"Okay, thanks." Aiden ended the call and hit the speed dial for Nia.

Bree rushed into the cottage. "What's going on?"

Scott put his arm around her. "Not sure yet."

Fiona rushed Bree, panting. "It's okay, girl." Bree glanced back and forth from Scott to Aiden. "It is okay, right?"

Aiden didn't answer. He focused on the phone call, waiting for Nia to pick up. Instead, it went to voice mail.

"No, no, no," Aiden said under his breath, marching to the front door and whipping it open. "Where are you, Nia?"

* * *

As Nia entered Healthy Eats restaurant on the outskirts of town, a woman in her late thirties greeted her from behind the counter. "Would you like a booth or table today?"

"A booth would be great, thanks," Nia said, thinking her brother would appreciate the privacy.

Nia had been relieved when she got the text from Danny asking her to join him for coffee. She'd worried all night, thinking maybe his boss's men had tracked him down and had hurt her brother.

Maybe Danny would finally tell her the whole story, because she sensed he'd left something out.

The hostess motioned Nia to a booth and placed a menu on the table. "Have you dined with us before?"

"No, I haven't." Nia slid the crutches into the booth. She'd decided to use them since she was going off resort property. "I've heard wonderful things about your place from some of our guests at Echo Mountain Resort."

"You work at the lodge?"

"Yes, I'm the concierge."

The woman extended her hand. "Nice to meet you. I'm Catherine, owner of Healthy Eats."

"Nia Sharpe."

"I think I've heard of you, the efficient woman who keeps things running at the resort." Catherine smiled.

"I didn't know my reputation was so grand."

"My brother, Nate, and your boss are friends. They meet here every week. I think it's the free coffee." She winked.

"I don't know about that. I've heard the food is amazing."

"What do you have a taste for today?" Catherine asked.

"I'll start with green tea, and maybe a muffin, something light?"

"How about I bring out some samples? Then you could recommend my place from firsthand experience."

"Sounds great."

With a smile, Catherine left Nia's table. Glancing out the

window, Nia wondered if taking off without telling anyone was such a good idea. It could cause grief and worry for her friends, especially Aiden. But Danny had asked her to come alone and she felt safe meeting him in a public place.

Besides, if she'd told Aiden, he would've demanded to come along. His opinion of her brother was already low, and Danny would never open up to her if Aiden were sitting across the table glaring at him.

Her phone rang and she dug it out of the side pocket of her purse. A blocked number popped up on the screen. It could be Danny.

"Hello?"

"Where are you?" Aiden demanded.

"Oh, hi, Aiden. I'm taking care of some things in town."

"Where in town?"

"What's wrong?"

"The alarm went off at the cottage. You must have triggered it when you left."

"No, I'm sure I set it."

"Where are you? *Exactly?*"

A prickly sensation crept up her neck. Not fear but anger.

"It's personal and I will be back later."

"After everything that's happened in the last—"

She hit the end button and stared at the phone. She'd just hung up on her boss, but what else could she do? She wasn't in the mood to be lectured to like a child, and she wouldn't tell him where she was because he'd race over and ruin her chance of seeing Danny one last time.

Sadness washed over her. Although her brother often frustrated her, she still loved him. Nothing changed the fact they were related by blood, and bound by history, and trauma.

"Green tea," Catherine said, sliding a flowered tea service onto the table. "Everything okay?"

Nia glanced at her. "Sure. Why do you ask?"

"You look…frustrated? Sorry, none of my business."

"It's okay. It's been a rough couple of days."

"The sweets should help. It'll be a few minutes."

The bell on the front door jingled and Nia glanced up, hopeful. It wasn't her brother. Will Rankin and his two little girls, both redheads, entered the restaurant. He spotted Nia and wandered over.

He introduced his daughters to her. "Claire, Marissa, you remember Nia."

"Hi there," Nia said with a bright smile.

"She's pretty. Why don't you marry her, Daddy?" the younger one said.

"You can't just marry anyone, Marissa. You have to be in love with them," Claire corrected her.

"No one's marrying anyone," Will said and smiled at Nia. "Sorry."

"Don't be. They're adorable."

"You want company?"

"Actually, I'm meeting someone."

"Okay, well, we'd better find a table. They're known for an early dinner rush here. Come on, girls." He shepherded them a few tables away. The younger girl, Marissa, glanced back at Nia and smiled. Nia waved back.

She checked her phone, wondering if she'd missed a text from Danny, but the only messages were from Aiden, ordering her to return to the resort ASAP.

Nia had learned to cope with Aiden's gruff and bossy exterior, but it had always been about work in the past, not about her personal life. She'd spent plenty of time with controlling men but didn't think Aiden was like the rest. He seemed to respect her, and would consider her thoughts and opinions.

Her knee-jerk reaction to his tone today proved that deep down she'd lumped him in with all the rest. And that wasn't fair. Aiden was better than that.

Catherine brought over a small plate of treats, and two more groups entered the restaurant. It was getting busy.

Nia glanced out the window in search of her brother, but there was no sign of him.

She sent another text, asking where he was.

He didn't respond. She decided to at least enjoy the sweets.

Half an hour later, when he still hadn't arrived, Nia grew worried.

Catherine waltzed over and motioned to the plate in front of Nia. "So, what did you think?"

"Oh, the sweets are delicious, thank you."

"Good. And don't be in a hurry to leave. It looks good when customers are waiting out front for a table. It builds buzz—at least, that's what my teenager tells me."

"Thanks."

The door jingled again. Nia looked up.

And recognized the tall, fortyish man who'd broken into her apartment last night. Wait a second. How was he free to walk around? Had he escaped the local lockup?

They made eye contact and she quickly looked away. Of all the places to eat in town, why was he here? He wouldn't do anything to her in public, would he?

Her gaze darted to Will's little girls, sitting only a few booths away, and then to a booth across the restaurant where a teenage couple held hands. Nia was putting all these people in danger by coming here.

She focused her attention out the window, shame warming her cheeks. Maybe Aiden was right. She shouldn't have left the cottage on resort grounds.

But she had, and now what should she do? She calmed her breathing and motioned to Catherine. Out of the corner of her eye, Nia caught sight of the tall man taking a seat at the counter.

Catherine approached Nia's table.

"I'll take the check, please," Nia said.

Catherine slid the check onto the table.

"Hang on." Nia dug in her purse for cash. She pulled out a twenty.

"Be right back," Catherine said.

Nia didn't dare make eye contact with the man at the counter. Her plan was to pay the bill and dash out of here. Right, she was going to dash on crutches?

Catherine returned with Nia's change. "It was nice meeting you."

"You, too." Nia got out of the booth and adjusted the crutches under her arms. "Where's your restroom?"

"In the back." She pointed.

"Thanks."

She wouldn't leave quite yet, but she'd remove herself from the room full of customers, lock herself in the bathroom and call for help. As she hobbled down the hall to the bathroom, she noticed a back door leading into the parking lot. Even better.

Heart pounding, she glanced over her shoulder. The man hadn't followed her. She pushed the door open and stepped outside, focused on getting to her car. A cool breeze drifted across her cheeks, making her shiver. Her crutches wobbled awkwardly on the gravel parking lot, so she decided to carry them and limp to her car.

She wondered if Danny had seen the man and taken off. Closing in on the car, she heard the creak of a door.

She glanced across the parking lot.

The man was jogging toward her. "Miss Sharpe?"

She fumbled in her purse for her keys. Why hadn't she taken them out before she'd left the restaurant?

"My name's Gus and I need to talk to you."

"Leave me alone!" she cried. Her eyes watered with fear, making it even harder to find her keys. Sensing that he was closing in, she flung out her crutch as a weapon.

"Stay away."

"I wanted to explain—"

"What, how you got out of jail after threatening my life?"

He put up his hands. "I wouldn't have hurt you. It's your brother I'm after."

"Well, he's not here, so why are you following me?"

"I wanted to apologize for scaring you last night. But Danny drives me crazy with all his lies."

"So that gives you the right to threaten me?"

"I was threatening to end him, not you."

"Nia?" Will called as he crossed the parking lot. "Everything okay?"

Nia glanced at Will, then at the restaurant. Will's daughters had plastered their faces against the window. The last thing she wanted was for them to see their father being brutalized.

"Stay back, Will," she said. "I'm fine."

"You don't look fine," he said.

"This is none of your business," Gus said.

"It is if you're upsetting my friend." Will approached the man from behind. "It seems like she wants you to leave her alone." Will grabbed Gus's arm and yanked him away.

Gus shoved Will, and Will shoved back. "Leave her alone," Will threatened, taking a step toward Gus.

With a nod, Gus looked as if he was going to leave peacefully. As he passed Will, Gus slugged him, and he fell to his knees. The sound of shrieking girls echoed from the restaurant.

Will started to get up.

"Stay down," Gus warned.

In that moment, Nia felt their fear, the same fear she'd felt as a child: the fear of brutality.

Nia gripped her right crutch with both hands and wound up. "Leave him alone!"

Ears ringing with adrenaline rushing through her body, Nia swung her crutch and nailed Gus in the back.

"Stop," he said. "I'm not going to hurt anybody."

She kept swinging, needing to get him away from Will. The howl of a siren mirrored the ringing in her ears as defensive instincts consumed her. The next few minutes were a blur.

Suddenly someone was there, dragging Gus away from Nia and Will. Yet she couldn't stop swinging the crutch.

A pair of strong yet gentle hands gripped her waist and pulled her against a firm body.

"Nia," Aiden said. "It's okay."

"He…hurt…Will," she gasped.

"He's okay, aren't ya, Will?"

Will stood up. "Yep, I'm good."

Through a haze of anger, Nia watched Will brush himself off.

"Nothing broken except my ego," Will said.

"Daddy!" his little girls cried, racing out of the restaurant.

Catherine chased after them. "I tried keeping them inside, Will."

The girls launched themselves at their dad and he offered a big hug in return.

His daughter Claire eyed the tall man as Nate escorted him to the patrol car.

"He should be in jail!" Claire cried.

"Yeah, he should be in jail!" Marissa echoed.

"Nia?" Aiden whispered against her ear. "It's okay. You can put the crutch down."

She was unable to let go, her fingers clutching the weapon as if she thought she might have to use it again.

Gus hesitated and glanced at Will then Nia. "I just need to talk to her."

Nate shoved the guy into the backseat and slammed the door.

"Nia?" Aiden said.

All the fight drained from her body and her legs buckled. Aiden scooped her up and put her in the passenger seat of her car. He shut the door and she closed her eyes.

She heard muffled discussion between Aiden and Nate

outside her window, although she couldn't hear what they were saying and she didn't much care. She was ashamed and embarrassed—ashamed that she'd brought trouble to the restaurant, exposing Will's girls to violence, and embarrassed that she'd gone a bit crazy just now, using her crutch as a weapon.

At this moment, she just wanted to disappear.

Someone tapped on the window. She opened her eyes and spotted Will's girls studying her with worried expressions. Just then, Aiden got in the car and turned on the engine so Nia could lower the window.

"Thank you for saving my dad," Claire said.

"Yeah, thank you for saving my dad," Marissa echoed.

"Sure."

"Okay, girls, I've gotta get Superhero Nia back home," Aiden said.

"'Bye, Superhero Nia," Claire said.

"'Bye, Superhero Nia," Marissa echoed.

With his hands on their shoulders, Will led the girls away from the car. Aiden pulled out of the lot. In the side-view mirror, Nia saw the girls wave. Nia stuck her hand out the window and waved back. Sadness washed over her. She could be responsible for potential nightmares about their dad being hurt.

"So, you went out to eat without telling me because…?" Aiden said.

Surprisingly he didn't sound angry or critical, just curious.

"My brother texted me, asking if I'd meet him."

Aiden frowned.

"I thought since it was a public place it would be safe." She shook her head. "Guess I'm an idiot."

"You're not an idiot. I just wish you would have let me tag along."

She studied his profile. "He wouldn't have confided in

me if you'd been there. It's obvious you don't like him, which would have made him uncomfortable."

"So, what did he say?"

"Nothing."

"Nia, look, I know I can be overbearing, but you've got to believe it comes from a place of caring. I need you to trust me, tell me about your secret meetings and what your brother says to you."

She glanced out the passenger window, hoping Danny was okay. "He never showed."

"Oh," Aiden said.

"How did you know where I was?"

"Nate's sister texted him that the famous concierge from Echo Mountain Resort was in her restaurant."

"A good thing she did."

"Yeah, I was just about to track the GPS on your phone."

"You were that worried?"

"I was."

"I'm sorry."

"Can I ask you a favor?" Aiden said.

"Sure."

"Please, never do that again."

"Leave without telling you?"

He nodded. "I think it took ten years off my life."

She reached out and placed her hand on his arm. "I was trying to be a good older sister."

"I understand, and I admire you for that, I do, but I wish you'd focus on taking care of yourself until this is resolved. Okay?"

"Okay."

A few minutes of silence stretched between them.

"I feel really bad," she said.

"What, are you hurt? How's the ankle?"

"The ankle's fine. I feel bad that I lost it back there."

"You were defending yourself."

"I embarrassed myself."

"I've found that people are a lot more forgiving than we give them credit for," he said.

"I guess." She thought for a second. "Is that why it's so important for you to protect me?"

"I'm not sure I understand the question."

"Because you haven't forgiven yourself for failing to protect someone you cared about?" She was pushing, she knew it, but she couldn't stop.

"Something like that."

"You say you've found people to be forgiving, yet you can't forgive yourself?"

"Let's not talk about me. Let's talk about you."

She studied the passing countryside.

"Did your brother indicate why he wanted to meet with you?"

"He sounded desperate, like he wanted to explain his situation."

"You got this from a text?"

"He wrote 'ASAP' and 'have to see you.'"

"And then he didn't show?"

She shook her head. "I hope he's okay."

"After everything you've been through because of him, you're still worried about his well-being?"

"He's still my brother."

"Well, you should know, your brother stole a lot more than two grand."

She glanced at him.

"Two hundred thousand," Aiden said.

"Oh, Danny." She sighed.

"However, the guy I tangled with outside Bree's cottage has nothing to do with your brother's situation."

"Well, that's a good thing, right?"

"I think so. It was a random attempted burglary of Bree's cottage, but he wasn't able to get in, so he was probably about to move on when I caught up with him."

They pulled onto Resort Drive.

"Nia?"

"Yes?"

"Why did you hang up on me?"

"That was insubordinate. I'm sorry."

"I'm asking as a friend, not your boss," he said.

"I was frustrated."

"Because I was worried about you?"

"Because you were being judgmental and condescending."

"That's how I sounded?" he said in a soft voice.

"Yes."

They drove the rest of the way to the cottage in silence. Nia considered explaining why his tone had set her off, but that would require a more in-depth explanation of her experience with men, both as a child and as an adult.

She simply didn't have the energy to get into that. Exhausted from events of the past hour, she wanted to flop down on a bed and shut herself off from the world.

Aiden pulled up to the cottage and parked. Before Nia could get a firm footing on the ground, Aiden was there, cupping her elbow to help her out.

"Thanks," she said.

Knowing it would make him feel better, she adjusted the crutches under her arms.

"Is she okay?" Bree called from the porch.

Aiden looked into her eyes. "Are you?"

She nodded that she was.

"She's good," Aiden called back. He stayed close as he escorted her up the steps and into his sister's cottage.

"We were so worried," Bree said, motioning them toward the kitchen. "What can I get you, Nia? Tea? Milk? Cookies?"

"I should probably lie down." She started for the stairs and Aiden blocked her.

"Here." He took the crutches from her and handed them

to Bree. "This will be quicker." He scooped Nia up in his arms yet again and made the climb to the second floor.

"Aiden, you don't have to—"

"Sure he does," Bree said.

Nia closed her eyes and leaned into him as he carried her into the spare room and placed her on the bed. "I need to check in at work, but I'll be back later, okay?" Aiden said.

"Sure, thanks."

As he left, he hesitated at the door. "If you decide to leave again for any reason—"

"I won't," she said.

With a nod, he brushed past his sister and went downstairs. A moment later the front door clicked shut.

Bree studied Nia from the bedroom doorway. "You meant it, about not going anywhere, right?"

"Yes."

"Good," Bree said. "I thought my brother was going to have a heart attack when we couldn't find you. I've never seen him like that." Bree paused, looking directly at Nia. "Ever."

For the next hour, rest eluded Nia as her brain kept replaying the scene from the restaurant parking lot. Finally she sat up and grabbed the Bible, hoping for something to ease the anxiety.

She found one of her favorite passages, Isaiah 41:10, and whispered the words.

"'So do not fear, for I am with you; do not be dismayed, for I am your God. I will strengthen you and help you; I will uphold you with my righteous right hand.'"

She took a deep, calming breath, letting the words wash over her.

The sound of a slamming door and deep, angry voices destroyed her momentary peace. She climbed off the bed and headed for the hallway.

"You can speak to her tomorrow," Aiden said.

"We'll talk to her tonight."

Nia turned the corner and spotted Aiden, with Scott by his side, facing off with a stranger in a blue suit. A second man came up behind the stranger.

"We have orders—"

"But not an arrest warrant," Scott said.

"We weren't planning to arrest her," the man in the blue suit said. "Unless you know something we don't."

Aiden took a step closer to the guy. "What I know is that she's been through enough these past two days and needs her rest."

"Aiden?" Nia said from the top of the stairs.

"Nia Sharpe?" The guy in the blue suit started for the stairs.

Aiden blocked him.

The guy shoved Aiden.

Aiden shoved back.

The guy in the blue suit spun Aiden around, pinning him against the wall and yanking his arms behind his back. "We can arrest you for interfering with a federal investigation."

"Stop! Let him go!" Frantic, Nia started down the steps a little too fast, and she lost her balance.

# EIGHT

Aiden elbowed the federal agent and shoved him back, then dived toward Nia to catch her before she tumbled down the entire flight of stairs.

His knee hit the edge of a stair as he focused on stopping her descent. It seemed as if it were happening in slow motion: Aiden scrambling to get to her, Nia waving her arms as if she was trying to grab on to something.

Almost there.

He caught her about midway down and pulled her against his chest, but he couldn't stop her momentum. The sharp edges of the stairs dug into his back as they slid down the rest of the way. He clenched his jaw against the pain, holding her in such a way that he'd bear the brunt of the fall.

They finally hit the floor with a thud.

"I'll call the resort doctor," Bree said.

"Stand back," Scott said to the agents. He knelt beside Aiden. "You okay?"

He was anything but okay. The guy who'd introduced himself as Agent John Nevins had threatened to arrest Aiden, which made Nia panic and lose her balance.

"Not sure," Aiden said. "But they need to leave."

Agent Nevins stepped into Aiden's line of sight. "We need to speak to both you and Miss Sharpe."

"Not tonight you won't. Give Scott your phone number and we'll call you tomorrow."

Scott motioned the men to leave.

"I'm sorry, Mr. McBride," Agent Nevins said. "I didn't mean for this to happen."

"This is a time-sensitive situation," the other agent, who'd said his name was Parker, protested.

"I understand," Scott said, encouraging them to leave. "I was on the job for ten years. But right now we need to tend to their injuries." The door shut with a click. A moment later, Scott knelt beside Aiden. "How's Nia?"

"Not sure. Nia?" Aiden brushed chestnut-colored hair away from her face.

She opened her warm brown eyes. "Now you see why I hate cops."

"Are you hurt?"

"I don't think so."

They were so close, closer than they'd ever been. He could feel the warmth from her breath against his skin. Even up close she was perfect.

"You didn't hit your head?" he asked.

"No."

She shifted off him and sat up. Stretching out her arms, and then her neck, she said, "Surprisingly, everything seems okay."

"You'll probably be sore tomorrow," Scott said.

"Dr. Spencer is on the way," Bree offered, kneeling beside Nia. "That was scary."

Aiden tried to sit up, but Nia placed her hand against his chest. "No, just say there until the doctor arrives."

"You got up."

"Please?"

He realized it was important to her that he remain still. "Okay."

"I can't believe you got those bullies to leave," Bree said.

"They're not bullies," Scott defended. "They're doing their job."

Bree planted her hands on her hips and glared at her boyfriend. "You're supposed to be on our side."

"I am, sweetheart. I'm always on your side." He leaned forward and kissed her cheek.

Nia glanced away, uncomfortable by the show of affection. Or maybe she was just sad that she'd never experience it for herself.

"Excuse me," Aiden said. "I could use some ice. If you're not too busy making out."

"Right, sorry." Bree dashed off toward the kitchen and Scott followed.

"I'll help," Scott said.

Aiden smiled at Nia. "Maybe you should make sure she doesn't get distracted."

"Oh no, if I leave, you'll try to get up and hurt yourself even worse."

"It's not that bad."

"Then what do you need the ice for?"

"An old football injury."

"Aiden," she said in a warning tone.

"Okay, fine. I might have banged my knee trying to get to you."

She glanced away, shame reddening her cheeks.

"Hey, hey." With his forefinger and thumb, he coaxed her to look at him again. "I don't like the sound of whatever you're thinking."

"How do you know what I'm thinking?"

"I can guess. I know you pretty well."

Aiden hadn't realized until now just how well he knew her. He knew that she took personal responsibility for so many things, including Aiden's well-being, which always puzzled him. What did he ever do to deserve her compassion?

"Here's the ice," Bree said, coming around the corner with a towel-wrapped ice bag.

Nia took it from her. "Okay, boss, where does this go?"

"Left knee."

When Nia placed the ice on his injury, he made sure not to wince or show any kind of reaction to the pain. He reached out to hold the ice securely over his knee and accidentally placed his hand over hers.

"Thanks," he said.

"I should be thanking you. You saved me from breaking my neck."

"You would have done the same for me," he teased.

She smiled and glanced at their hands. "Yeah, you're probably right."

The next morning Aiden awoke in Bree's cottage sore from the tumble down the stairs. After Dr. Spencer checked him out and said he was okay but should go for X-rays, Aiden planted himself on the couch, determined to stay close and protect Nia.

Sure, a protector with a bum knee and sore back and neck. It was the second night in a row he'd spent on Bree's lumpy couch instead of in his own bed, but he didn't mind. His place was lonely anyway and the nightmares didn't seem to plague him at Bree's place.

Standing, he tested the knee, which didn't hurt as much as he'd expected it to. His phone buzzed with a call.

"McBride," he answered.

"It's Nate. Thought you'd want to know—Gus Chambers wasn't charged."

"What, is this guy made of Teflon? Wasn't he charged with assaulting Will?"

"Witnesses said it was a shoving match on both their parts, so no. The good news is, Gus is leaving town."

"Yeah, I'll believe that when he's gone."

"How's Nia?"

"Almost broke her neck falling down the stairs thanks to a late-night visit from the feds."

"They were supposed to check in with me first."

"Guess they can't follow directions."

"Did they question you?"

"I sent them away. Said I'd be in touch."

"Okay, well, call if you need me."

"Thanks." Aiden ended the call and shuffled into the kitchen.

"You walk like you're ninety," Bree said, leaning against the counter drinking coffee.

He hip-bumped her out of his way. "You're bad for my ego."

"That's my job as your little sister." She handed him a mug.

He poured a cup of coffee. "Nia asleep?"

"Nope. She's been up since dawn, putting final touches on some family reunion and coordinating temporary accommodations for mud slide victims."

"Wait—she left the cottage?"

"Relax. She did it by phone."

"But it's only…" He glanced at the clock. It read eight-thirty.

"You let me sleep in?"

"Not me—Nia. She said you needed the rest. I wanted to wake you at six."

"Where is she?"

"On the front porch with the two agents from last night."

He nearly spit out his coffee. "What?" He started to go to Nia, but Bree grabbed his arm.

"Hang on, big brother. It was her idea. She asked Scott for Agent Nevins's number and called him."

"I'd better go check on her."

His sister wouldn't release him. "Do you have faith in Nia?"

"Of course."

"Then show her."

"What…? I don't understand."

"Don't go out there guns blazing. Be calm and support-ive, not bossy and irritable."

"She doesn't like cops. She doesn't trust them." He glanced

toward the front of the house. "Why would she meet with the agents alone?"

"To protect you."

"Me?" He snapped his attention to Bree.

"She probably doesn't want them arresting you like they tried to last night, because with your attitude, you're asking for it."

Bree's phone buzzed on the counter and she eyed it. "It's a SAR text. Since they didn't find anything yesterday, they're enlisting K9 teams to search for the missing federal agents."

"You and Fiona go ahead," he said, limping toward the front door.

"You should ask to borrow Nia's crutches while you're out there," she teased.

"Maybe I will."

Aiden reached the front door and hesitated. Bree was right. If he stepped outside with a chip on his shoulder he'd only make things worse for Nia. And that was something he definitely didn't want to do. But resentment about how the agents had acted last night simmered low in his gut. Somehow he had to release it.

"Dear God, don't let me do anything stupid," he whispered. "I just want to help her."

He took a deep breath, opened the door and joined them on the front porch.

"Good morning." Aiden extended his hand to the lead agent who'd tried to arrest him. "Sorry about last night."

The agent, who'd introduced himself last night as John Nevins, returned the gesture.

"Please accept my apologies, as well," Agent Nevins said. "This case is complicated and frustrating."

"Mr. McBride," the second agent greeted him.

"Agent Parker, right?" Aiden said.

"Yes, sir, Rick Parker."

They also shook hands.

"You guys need something to drink?" Aiden asked. "My sister makes an amazing cup of coffee."

"We're good, thanks," Agent Nevins said.

"Would you mind if I hung around? You've probably figured out that I'm protective of Nia. She's my best employee. The resort would crumble without her."

Nia glanced down at the wooden floorboards, but he couldn't tell if her expression was one of embarrassment or disappointment. Did she dislike him referring to her as an employee?

"Actually, you might be helpful since you seem to have been around when much of this happened," Agent Nevins said and then shot an apologetic frown at Aiden. "Wait—I didn't mean for that to sound like an accusation."

"I didn't take it as one," Aiden said.

"Good. Miss Sharpe was giving us a rundown about what's happened over the past few days. We're concerned about Agents Brown and McIntyre not returning from the mountains."

"It's rugged terrain out there. If you're not an experienced hiker, you could find yourself in a world of trouble," Aiden said.

Bree bounded out of the house with Fiona beside her. "Headed to the command center. See ya later."

"Be careful," Aiden said.

"You, too." His sister's golden retriever hopped into the front seat of her truck and they took off.

"So, back to your missing agents," Aiden said. "May I ask why they were looking for me?"

"They said they were following a money trail that led here, to Echo Mountain Resort," Agent Parker said. "They had identified you, Mr. McBride, as a suspect in an international drug ring."

"What?" Nia snapped. "That's ridiculous."

Aiden leaned against the house for support. "How did they come to that conclusion?"

"Emails sent by Danny Sharpe to your account at the resort."

"I never received any emails."

"Aiden would never do anything illegal, and don't you try to frame him for anything," Nia defended.

Agent Parker put up his hands. "We're not framing anyone for anything."

"But you think I'm some kind of drug runner?" Aiden said.

"The agents were following the evidence. Maybe the email landed in your spam folder?"

"I received an email, one I found just the other day," Nia offered. "But it was just a link, so I assumed Danny's email had been hacked."

Agent Parker looked at Nia. "Your brother was a drug courier. Agents Brown and McIntyre suspected him of disappearing with proceeds from a sale instead of turning it in to the cartel he was working for."

"A drug cartel," Nia whispered. "Danny, what have you gotten yourself into?"

"When he went off the grid, the agents thought he'd been killed by cartel thugs. They pulled his phone records and found the emails and multiple calls made to Echo Mountain Resort. They said that's why they were headed out here, to speak to the manager."

"They challenged Aiden's exemplary military record," Nia said. "They were trying to intimidate me."

"I'm sorry about that," Agent Nevins said.

"Hang on," Aiden said, curious. "What *aren't* you telling us?"

Agent Nevins hesitated. "There have been recent indications that Agents Brown and McIntyre may have gone rogue. At any rate, we need to find them."

"You mean they're corrupt?" Aiden said.

"It's possible, yes."

"I was right not to trust them." Nia glanced up at Aiden.

"If they thought you were involved in hiding drug money, they would have done anything to find it. Even hurt you."

Aiden placed his hand on her shoulder for comfort.

"They don't know we suspect them of anything," Agent Parker said. "Please keep that to yourselves. We need to find them ASAP, before they either figure out our suspicions or get the money from Danny and dispose of the evidence."

"You mean kill him," Nia said.

"Your brother is critical to resolving this case," Nevins said. "If the agents couldn't track down the money through Mr. McBride, they would have gone after Danny directly."

"They thought I was hiding the money at the resort?" Aiden said.

"Possibly, which is why they wanted to find you. Would you mind if we looked into your accounts, just to cover all our bases?"

"You won't find anything," Nia said.

"I'll have to check with the owner of the property for permission," Aiden said. "But he shouldn't have a problem with that."

"In the meantime, Danny is the key to finding Agents Brown and McIntyre." Nevins glanced at Nia. "Did your brother give you any indication where he was headed next?"

"He said he was going home to pay back his boss, but that was obviously a lie. Wait—why did he need money from me if he has all this drug money?"

"If the bills were marked or identifiable in any way, he wouldn't want to use them," Agent Nevins said.

A small pickup truck pulled into the driveway and Dr. Kyle Spencer stepped out. Dr. Spencer—or Spence, as he liked to be called—had recently moved to Echo Mountain and hadn't wasted any time joining the search-and-rescue team. The team appreciated the doctor's skills, and the single females appreciated a new bachelor in town. The clean-cut, handsome physician had caused quite a stir when he'd arrived, although Aiden sensed the man wasn't interested in romance.

"Good morning," Spence said, eyeing the agents. "Everything okay?"

"These are Agents Nevins and Parker from the FBI. They're investigating the missing agents," Aiden explained.

"I'm on my way to the command site but wanted to check on my patient first. How's the knee, Aiden?"

"Still working."

"Good. I brought you this." Spence pulled a brace out of a plastic bag. "Wear it."

Aiden must have made a face because Nia said, "I'll make sure he does."

"And you could probably use a stronger wrap for your ankle, Nia."

"Yeah, since she refuses to use the crutches," Aiden countered.

Spence redirected his attention to Aiden. "Wouldn't hurt you to get a CT scan on that head of yours."

"It's fine. No headache, nausea or anything indicating a concussion," Aiden said.

"Is that so, Dr. McBride?" Spence jabbed.

"You said you were headed to the command site?" Nevins asked the doctor.

"I am."

"Mind if we follow you?"

"No, although you won't be allowed to accompany our teams into the mountains. Only trained volunteers are allowed on missions."

"But we could help."

"Sorry, but we can't risk you becoming victims and giving us two more bodies to haul down the mountain."

"All the same, we'd like to be close when you find our men."

"I understand." Spence narrowed his eyes at Aiden. "You'd better be wearing that brace by the time I get back."

"Will do."

"Thanks for your help." Agent Nevins turned to Nia. "You've got my number in case you hear from your brother or you think of anything else that might be helpful."

"Yes, sir," she said. "Wait—what about interrogating the man who threatened me at my apartment? He's involved in this somehow."

"We did. He's after Danny for something unrelated to our case."

The three men took off for the command post in the mountains.

Nia stood but didn't make eye contact with Aiden. "Let's go inside and get that brace on your knee."

As she passed him, he reached for her hand and inter- laced their fingers. "Nia? What's going on in that head of yours?"

She glanced into his eyes. "They suspected you of being a drug courier—" she paused "—because of my brother."

She shook her head, pulled her hand from his and went into the house. Aiden followed. "But I'm not involved with drugs and they know that."

"Still…" She motioned him to a thick-cushioned chair. "Take a seat and I'll help you with the brace."

He was about to say he was perfectly capable of doing it himself, but thought better of it. He wanted to stay close, maybe even get her to articulate her frustrations so they wouldn't eat away at her. She had to be incredibly disap- pointed in her brother right now.

He took off his boot and stretched his leg out on the sofa. Handing her the brace, he said, "Thanks for offer- ing to help."

"It's the least I can do considering all the trauma I've caused you and your family."

As if she just realized what she'd said, she froze and looked at him. He'd never get tired of gazing into those warm brown eyes.

"Are you…? Have you been sleeping okay?" she asked.

"Sure. Why?"

"I thought…" She hesitated, focusing on adjusting the brace. "I mean, with everything that's been happening, you might…you know…"

Right, trigger more nightmares.

Yet except for the one he'd had outside her apartment the other day, the nightmares had been less frequent, actually, ever since she'd pounded on his cottage door and awakened him from an unusually violent one. He'd never forget the look on Nia's face when he'd answered, a horrified look. Aiden's expression had probably terrified her.

"I should get to work," he said as he finished strapping on the brace.

"I'm going with you," she said.

"I don't think that's a good idea."

"I can't sit here all day and night, Aiden. I've got work to do. Besides, I'm more isolated and at risk here at the cottage than if I'm surrounded by a resort full of people…" She hesitated. "Unless you think I'm putting them at risk, too."

"I doubt it. Drug thugs like things quick and easy. They'd avoid a resort crowd."

"Good. Then it's settled. They probably need my help with the mud slide victims in the barn."

"I'll come with you."

"Aiden, you're the big boss. You've got things to do. You can't hover around me day and night."

"You said it—I'm the boss. Therefore, I can do whatever I want."

The day flew by, Nia managing the needs of residents in the barn, helping them find more comfortable temporary housing until their neighborhoods were deemed safe.

There were fewer displaced residents than originally expected, but even twelve people were plenty to keep Nia busy. She helped them in any way she could.

She sensed Aiden's presence every now and then, catching sight of him speaking with an employee or giving orders over his radio. It wasn't until midday that she realized if Aiden weren't around, Scott or Harvey would be close by. It seemed that Aiden had assigned Nia her own protection detail.

It felt good to work because it kept her mind off this mess she'd brought to the resort, to Aiden's life. And here she thought her brother would repay the two grand and all would be right with the world. How naive on her part.

When the clock struck six, Aiden asked her to join him for dinner in his office. They shared a meal of salmon and mixed vegetables, discussing guest requests and special events.

A police officer stopped by to say he was done dusting for prints in her office. He hovered in the doorway instead of coming into the office, acting as if he was interrupting a private affair. Nia blushed, enjoying the few seconds of misunderstanding. She liked the thought of being Aiden's girlfriend.

That was when she knew she had to excuse herself.

She downed the rest of her tea and stood. "Thanks for dinner."

"I'll walk you back to the cottage."

"Actually, I promised Tripp I'd check with him at the front desk before I called it a night."

"Take the crutches."

"Okay, Doc." She adjusted them beneath her arms. It made Aiden feel better that she used them, so she wouldn't argue.

"I don't want you going anywhere alone," Aiden said. "I'll walk you up front."

Aiden's desk phone rang. "McBride...What? The whole system is down or just the south wing?...My tech didn't say anything about...That's unacceptable."

As his voice rose in pitch, Nia felt the need to distance

herself and give him privacy. She stepped out into the hall and debated walking to the front desk. No, she wouldn't go against Aiden's wishes.

"Hey, Nia," Scott said, heading in her direction. "What are you doing out here?"

"Aiden's on a call, so I wanted to give him privacy."

"This should have been fixed two days ago!" Aiden's angry voice drifted into the hall.

"Probably about the security system," Scott said. "How's the ankle?"

"Better, thanks. And thanks for keeping an eye on me today."

Scott feigned innocence. "I'm not sure I know what you're referring to."

"Thanks anyway."

He smiled. "Sure. I'll catch you later."

"Good night."

Scott left through the staff door. It banged shut behind him.

She decided rather than stand idle, she'd check her office. It wasn't far from Aiden's, and if she hovered in the doorway, he could see her from the hall.

Heading for her office, she braced herself for what she'd see once she peeked inside.

The lights suddenly went out, drowning her in darkness.

"Nia!" Aiden called.

Someone gripped her arm.

She gasped for breath.

A male voice whispered in her ear, "Don't make a sound."

# NINE

"Nia!" Aiden's voice bellowed from down the hall.

"Don't even think about it," the man threatened. "I don't want to hurt him but I will."

Her pulse pounding in her ears, she nodded her understanding. He yanked her back, away from her office, away from the hall leading to Aiden's office. With a firm grip of her arm, he pulled her into a nearby storage closet.

No, God, please don't let her die this way, at the hands of a criminal in a closet just around the corner from Aiden's office. He'd never forgive himself, and she still had so much good work to do on this earth.

The closet door shut with a soft click. She felt her way to the corner, using the crutches as a guide. She knew this closet. It was where they kept office and party supplies for special events. She headed for a shelf where they kept scissors, thinking she could use a weapon right about now, except the man could easily overpower her, using the weapon on Nia. Maybe not such a good idea.

"Sit down," he said.

She collapsed and hugged her knees, feeling so utterly vulnerable.

A small light clicked on.

Sitting across the storage closet was the agent from the other day, the one calling himself Greg Brown.

"You're alive," she said.

He winced as he positioned himself across from her. "I need to find your brother."

"I don't know where he is."

"I don't believe you." He was sweating and clutching his side.

"Where's your partner?" she asked.

Feet pounded in the hallway just outside the closet. The emergency lights must have come on.

"Nia!" Aiden's voice echoed through the door.

She heard a click and glanced at Greg. He gripped a gun in his hand. It wasn't pointed at her, but she didn't miss the threat. She noticed blood on his hand.

"You're bleeding," she said.

"Do you and your brother share a bank account?" he said.

"No, I wouldn't be that foolish."

"Why did he come out here?"

"He said he wanted to get a job and earn money to pay off his employer."

A pained chuckle escaped Greg's lips. "Get a job, right."

She decided to keep talking to him in a normal tone in the hopes he'd come to his senses and let her go. She was not the enemy, nor was she involved in Danny's business. "Sounds like you know him pretty well."

"Obviously not well enough or I would have seen this coming."

"Seen what coming?"

"The betrayal."

"You too, huh?" *Bond with him, Nia. That will help.*

"When things calm down out there, you'll need to come with me," he said.

"Why? I have nothing to do with Danny's business."

"I can't keep chasing him, but he'll come to me if I've got his sister."

She'd let him think she'd go willingly off resort property with him, yet somehow she'd escape.

"Don't do anything stupid or I'll shoot that boyfriend of yours."

"I don't have a boyfriend."

"Nia! She was just here," Aiden said to someone, probably Scott.

"He sounds like a boyfriend," Greg said with a smirk.

She decided to turn the tables. After all, she knew he wouldn't hurt her if he planned to use her as bait.

"Why did you turn corrupt?" she said.

He didn't answer, just stared at her. A few seconds later he said, "Who told you that?"

"No one needed to tell me anything. You've kidnapped me and are threatening me with a gun. A federal agent wouldn't do that."

"You'd be surprised what a federal agent would do." He cracked open the door to see into the hallway.

Nia took the opportunity to grab scissors off the shelf behind her. Could she do it? Could she really stab a man, a man she knew was already injured? No, she'd have to figure out something else.

"On the count of three, you head for the staff exit and I'll follow. Get up." He eyed the hallway and then motioned her into the doorway. "One, two, three."

She took a few steps out of the closet, spun around and swung the crutch at the agent. Greg put up his hands in self-defense and then tried grabbing the crutch. She managed to pull away and nail him in the stomach. He stumbled backward into the dark storage room. She took off down the hall, clinging to the crutches but not using them.

The door to the employee entrance opened. Aiden and Scott entered in a full sprint.

"Nia!" Aiden called, rushing up to her. He caught her in his arms just as she thought she might collapse.

"Storage closet. He's got a gun" was all she could get out.

"Get her out of here," Scott ordered.

"But—"

"Go!" Scott snapped at Aiden.

"It's one of the missing agents," Nia said. "He threatened me."

"Just go. I'll handle this." Scott motioned them away.

Aiden led Nia outside into the cool night air. His radio beeped. "McBride," he answered. "Have them come to the employee entrance when they get here," Aiden said.

Aiden escorted Nia to a nearby wooden bench and knelt beside her. "Police are on the way. Are you hurt?"

She shook her head. "I'm okay. He wanted to use me as bait for Danny."

"But you're really okay?" He squeezed her hand.

"Yes. He didn't hurt me."

"I am so sorry."

"Thank you."

"It's my fault. If my security system was working properly, if—"

"Don't." She pressed her fingertips against his lips. A moment of awareness sparked between them. She'd never touched him in such an intimate way, but she had to stop him from beating himself up. "I should be the one apologizing since it's my brother that brought all this trouble down on us. You sure you don't want me to move away and take all this with me?"

"If you leave, this place will fall apart."

Aiden wanted to say he'd fall apart, but this was not the time to let emotions take over, especially since she needed him to be strong, not needy and weak. Only a strong man could protect her.

"No concierge is irreplaceable, Aiden," she said.

He glanced into her shuttered brown eyes. If he kept referring to her as *just* an employee, he'd lose her for sure.

"The guests aren't the only ones who would suffer from losing an exceptional concierge," he started, edging dangerously close to the line. "Your church community and friends would suffer if you abandoned them."

"But I would be protecting you."

"And who would protect you, Nia? You'd be out there,

all alone, running from men who could overpower you..."
He paused. "And hurt you."

He shook his head, glancing at their entwined fingers.
They were still holding hands.

As if she feared his discomfort at the intimate touch, she
slipped her hand from his.

"I don't want to argue with you," he said. "But I'm worried about you. You've been through a traumatic event and
it can cause delayed effects."

"I told you, I'm fine," she said.

"You should see Spence."

"I don't need a doctor."

Aiden heard police cars pull up behind them and a door
slam. "Where is he?" Nate Walsh asked.

"Storage room on the left about fifty feet from the exit,"
Aiden said, but didn't take his eyes off Nia.

She glanced over his shoulder. "There's an ambulance.
Oh no, Scott—"

"Shh," Aiden comforted her. "They probably sent it as
a precaution."

Nate rushed inside with another cop. Aiden shifted onto
the bench beside Nia and pulled her against his chest. He
felt a half second of resistance, but then she relaxed and
leaned into him.

He instinctively stroked her arm, hoping to keep her
calm.

A few minutes later, two paramedics wheeled a stretcher
out of the building, Nate hovering beside it.

Nia sat straight. "What happened? Is Scott okay?"

"I'm fine," Scott said, wandering over to where Aiden
and Nia were seated. "The agent was suffering from a gunshot wound to his side."

"The blood on his hand," Nia whispered.

"I guess when you hit him to get away, you hit the bull's-eye."

"His wound?"

"Yep. He was unconscious when I got to him."

"Scott!" Bree cried, launching herself into his arms. Fiona danced around their legs, barking excitedly.

"I'm fine, honey," Scott said.

Nia's eyes widened as she stared at the stretcher. The reality of what had happened hit home, and her entire body started trembling.

"Shh, it's okay," Aiden said, holding her tight. "You're okay now."

"But…I did that. I k-k-k-illed him?"

Aiden glanced at Scott.

"He was still breathing," Scott offered.

"Hear that, sweetheart? He's still alive," Aiden said. "He probably passed out from blood loss."

"I noticed blood…on his hand." Her trembling intensified.

"We need to get her to the hospital," Aiden said to Scott and Bree.

"No, no hospital," Nia argued. "I'm not hurt. Please, Aiden."

"Let's get her to the car," Scott said.

"No hospital," Nia said, more insistent.

"We'll take you back to Bree's," Aiden said. "Okay? No hospital."

Nia nodded against him. He picked her up and then eyed his sister. "Crutches?"

"Got 'em."

Aiden carried Nia to the truck and set her in the bench seat between him and Scott.

"I'll meet you at the cottage," Bree said.

"Wait—call Spence," Aiden said. "See if he's back from the mission."

"Will do."

Scott pulled away, heading for the cottage.

"Agents Nevins and Parker are going to want to talk to her," Scott said.

"Tomorrow," Aiden said.

"Their agent's been shot. They may not want to wait until tomorrow. They'll probably show up at the cottage."

"Then let's set her up at Quinn's apartment for the night. That way, they won't know where she is."

Scott took a left and headed for the private residence.

Quinn, the resort owner, was on a business trip, so he shouldn't mind if they used his apartment for Nia. They'd left him a message about the break-in and would need to debrief him about the rogue agent in his storage closet. But that could wait. The last thing Nia needed was to relive tonight's trauma by retelling every detail to the agents.

Again, Aiden worried that they'd arrest him for interfering with an investigation, but his primary concern was Nia. Keeping her safe, helping her cope with the trauma of the past few days.

Scott pulled up to the private garage and Aiden reached for the truck door.

"No," Nia said, clinging to him.

She was still trembling and it drove him nuts.

"I need to open the garage door. Be right back."

He begrudgingly removed her hands from his body. He got out of the truck and punched in the code on the side of the garage, scanning the property, paranoid about any number of bad guys following them and hurting Nia.

Scott pulled into the garage and Aiden helped Nia out of the truck. He picked her up yet again, and Scott came around to open the door to the apartment. They flipped on a few lights.

"Where are we?" Nia asked.

"Quinn's apartment. You need peace and quiet."

He settled her on the living room sofa and adjusted some throw pillows at one end.

Scott hovered close by, awaiting further instruction.

"Why don't you lie down?" Aiden said to Nia.

She nodded and stretched out on the sofa.

"I'll make you some tea," he said.

She grabbed his hand and squeezed.

"I'll be right there," he said, pointing to the kitchen, not fifteen feet away.

She slowly released him, his fingers burning from the warmth of her touch. He nodded for Scott to join him in the kitchen. Aiden filled the teapot and put it on the stove, then turned to Scott.

"This is unacceptable, Scott. Our key-card system isn't fully functional, and it hasn't been fixed for days. And how did the guy cut the power? We can't provide a safe environment if we don't have our act together."

Scott planted his hands on his hips and glanced at the floor. "I know. I'm sorry."

"I'm not blaming you, but I'm frustrated."

"I'll take care of it, sir."

"You don't have to call me 'sir.' We're way past that."

Scott glanced at him. "I feel responsible."

"So do I, so does Nia. How about we all stop drowning in guilt and fix the problem before it happens again? First, we need the security system up and running ASAP. Make whatever calls you need to make, wake people up and solve this problem. We should also increase security personnel. It can't be you and part-time Harvey, not as long as Nia's life is in danger. I've got a list of people I trust, people with law-enforcement backgrounds. I want two men working twelve-hour shifts for total coverage. Technically, they'll be hired as maintenance officers. Third, you were a cop. Use those detective skills to anticipate their next move."

"Kind of hard when we don't even know who 'they' are."

Aiden found the tea and plopped a bag into a mug. "Let's assume the drug cartel sent thugs to find Danny and get their money back."

"And Danny led them directly to his sister. Nice," he said sarcastically.

"I have a feeling Danny doesn't think beyond his own

needs. So, let's assume he's left town. The threat should follow him, right?"

"Not if they don't know where he went. They'll keep mining their contacts."

"You mean Nia?"

"Unfortunately, yes. It would help to know how those first two federal agents fit into this."

"Agents Nevins and Parker said there's a good chance they're corrupt."

"Really?" Scott said, leaning against the counter.

"You sound surprised." The kettle whistled. Aiden took it off the stove and poured hot water into the mug.

"I'm surprised they'd share that kind of information with you."

"We are their only leads in this case—or Nia is, anyway—so they're keeping us in the loop."

"Well, you'll be safe here. Although, it wouldn't be the worst idea in the world to take her someplace even more remote."

"I know." Aiden ran a hand through his hair.

"But you've got a resort to run—"

"It's not that. I can manage things by phone for a few days."

"What, then?"

"I'm not sure I'm the best person to protect her."

"I disagree. You're a natural at protecting that woman."

Scott's phone buzzed and he answered. "This is Scott. Yes?…Okay, I'll be right there." He pocketed his phone. "Good news. The IT guy, Zack, thinks he found what's wrong with the key-card system. Wants me to come to his office."

"Good. That's one problem off the list." Aiden walked him to the front door. "Check in later."

"Will do." Scott left the apartment.

Aiden went back to the kitchen, trying not to look at Nia on the sofa. Shame coursed through him at the thought that he'd let her down again. If only he hadn't answered the phone, if only he'd been paying attention to her when she'd wandered off.

As he dunked the tea bag, the sound of Nia's frantic voice echoed from the living room. "No, please…stop!"

Aiden darted around the corner and saw Nia thrashing on the sofa, her fingers digging into the cushions beneath her.

He swiftly crossed the room and reached for her.

"Don't hurt me. Please don't hurt me," she cried, swinging her arms and smacking him in the face with her hand.

"Nia, it's me. It's Aiden." He gripped her arms and looked deeply into her eyes. "Wake up, sweetheart. You had a bad dream."

With a gasp, she blinked a few times and her expression changed from fear to understanding. She stopped flailing, and he pulled her against his chest.

"You're okay. You're safe."

He held her close for a few minutes, rocking slightly. He hoped he was doing this right, that the motion and pressure of his arms around her back would comfort her.

"That's so embarrassing," she finally whispered.

"No, it's not. It's normal. You've been through a traumatic experience."

"I wasn't dreaming about tonight."

"What, then?"

She broke the hold and leaned back against the sofa. He thought she meant to put distance between them, but instead she settled her cheek against his shoulder. He put his arm around her and heard a sigh escape her lips.

"My stepfather," she said. "Why would I be dreaming about him? It's been years. I put all that behind me."

"The past has a way of resurfacing when we're in an emotionally charged state."

"Aiden…" She hesitated. "Your nightmares—have they been more frequent lately?"

"Actually, no."

"Come on," she pressed.

"I'm serious. I think that protecting you is forcing me to face my trauma head-on."

"I feared it would make things worse."

"Nothing could be worse than seeing you hurt."

"Yeah, you'd have a hard time replacing me at the resort, I know."

He closed his eyes, wishing he could say the words, tell her that she meant so much more to him than an employee. But getting emotionally tangled up in knots wouldn't help him protect her. On the contrary, it would only distract him.

Aiden knew it might help if she were to talk about her nightmare. Hadn't the counselor encouraged Aiden to do that very thing? Talk about his fears and his shame? It never seemed to work completely for Aiden, nor did prayer. He held on to his pain with an ironclad grip and that tension imprisoned his heart.

He didn't want Nia to suffer the same way, so he decided to get her talking.

"Did you ever get help?" he asked.

"You mean…?"

"About your stepfather."

"He was a cop. No one would believe us."

"I meant afterward. Did you see a counselor?"

"Yes, a few years ago, when I was working in Spokane. It was about the time my mom died. I went back for the funeral—" she hesitated "—and I saw Walter. I thought I'd moved past it, but the nightmares started up again and it was affecting my productivity at work."

"Did counseling help?"

"Very much so. Her name was Rosalie. Not only was she a counselor, but she also belonged to my church, so we integrated prayer into my sessions. It was wonderful." She tipped her head back and studied him. "What about you?"

"What about me?"

"Have you ever talked to anyone?"

"Sure, but it didn't do much good, as you've obviously figured out by now."

"I don't think we're ever completely healed, Aiden. Those scars are the ones that make us stronger."

She placed her cheek against his shoulder yet again. "You know what I think really helped me?"

"What?"

"The prayer part. When I pray, I'm opening my heart to God. I'm not demanding, or expect anything in return. But I always feel that much closer to a state of grace, ya know?"

He didn't, but he wasn't sure how to say that without offending her.

"When we were in the mountains you made a comment about not being worthy of God's love," she said. "Why would you think that?"

"Let's just say I've disappointed Him one too many times."

"God is about love and forgiveness, Aiden."

"I haven't forgiven myself. Why would He?"

She leaned back again to search his eyes. He felt so vulnerable when she looked at him this way, with compassionate and caring eyes.

"Why can't you forgive yourself?" she asked. "Maybe I can help."

"I should be comforting you, not dumping my problems in your lap."

"Please? It will make me feel better to be able to help you." She pulled away from him, but held on to his hand. "It's about your friend Yates, right?"

He really didn't want to do this.

She squeezed his hand. "It's okay. Tell me."

"We were on foot patrol in a village," he started. "My bum knee kept me back. He went ahead. He was killed. End of story."

"And you blame yourself?"

"It should have been me."

"I'm so sorry."

"Yeah, well, I have a way of letting people down."

"Who else have you let down?"

He shook his head.

"Aiden, talk to me. Who did you let down?"

"My dad. The last time we spoke, before I left on my tour of duty, we argued." He found himself tracing his finger over the back of her hand. It comforted him somehow. "Dad said I was making a mistake by joining the army. He thought I should have gone for more surgery, tried to stay in football, get a scholarship or something."

"You didn't want to?"

"The prognosis was pretty grim. They couldn't fix me, so I chose to do something else that I thought would make Dad proud. Instead, we got into this huge fight, me accusing him of trying to control me, him accusing me of running from my problems. It was bad."

"And he passed away while you were overseas?"

Aiden nodded. "Heart attack. I didn't get a chance to tell him I just wanted him to be proud of me. To apologize."

"It's never too late," she said.

"He's gone. It's too late."

She squeezed his hand. "Do you trust me?"

He searched her lovely brown eyes. "Yes."

"Then pray with me."

"I don't know any prayers."

"It's okay—I do." She closed her eyes, but didn't release his hand. "Dear God, please help Aiden open his heart to self-forgiveness, and to peace. He's a kind, loving and protective brother, son and friend, and he's struggling to find his way back to You."

As she spoke the words, Aiden remarked on how amazing this woman was. With everything that had happened to her in the past few days, she was less worried about herself and more concerned about his wounded heart.

"He needs You, Lord. He needs Your strength, Your guidance. And Your love." She opened her eyes.

"Amen," they said in unison.

It had been years since he'd participated in any type of prayer other than at mealtime, and saying "Amen" with Nia sent a rush of hope through his chest.

"That was…nice," he said. "Although Bree might disagree about the 'kind' part."

She cracked a smile, making him want to take her in his arms again. The air hummed between them, as if her prayer had opened up the possibilities to an amazing kind of love shared between a man and a woman. A kind of love he had never allowed himself to feel before.

"Nia," he whispered. It was a plea, but for what?

Her phone suddenly went off, breaking the moment.

"You'd better get that," Aiden said.

"Yeah." But she didn't move to answer.

"It might be important."

With a reluctant nod, she took the call.

"Hello?…Danny?" She glanced at Aiden. "What? Who's trying to kill you?…Danny, slow down and tell me where you are," she said in a demanding, motherly tone. "No, don't…Danny!"

# TEN

The line went dead.

"Danny!" Nia cried, desperate for him to come back on the line. But he was gone. She stood. "We've got to help him."

"Hang on." Aiden touched her arm. "Nia, stop. Think about this."

She took a few steps away from him and grew light-headed, probably still suffering the aftereffects of tonight's kidnapping. Leaning into the dining room table, she said, "I've never heard him sound like that before. He was terrified."

Aiden tentatively reached out and touched her arm. "Where was he calling from?"

Her eyes watered. "He didn't say, only that he was close and needed my help. And then…"

"And then, what?"

"He said 'they're here' and the line went dead." She limped away from him. "We have to find him, Aiden."

"And we will. I'll call Nate. Maybe he can help. Would you please sit down?"

"I can't. I need to do something. I need to go look for him, something."

"Nia, do you trust me?"

She looked into his tender blue eyes. "Of course."

"Then let me handle this. You can't go out there blindly looking for your brother. You'll make yourself a target. Please? Relax on the sofa?"

He was right. What could she possibly do in the dark, with a bull's-eye pinned to her back?

Aiden made the call. "Nate, it's Aiden. Nia got a call from Danny and he sounded like he was in trouble…No, he didn't say where, only that he was close. Can you— understand. Okay, thanks."

He pocketed his phone.

"What did he say?"

"He's stuck at the hospital, but he'll call when he's free."

"Right, because my brother is a suspected criminal, it's not a priority. I get it." She started to get up again.

He took her hand. "Nia, that's not it. This is a small town with limited police resources. They have to deal with what's in front of them."

"You'd think they'd want to find Danny."

"They do, but not as much as Agents Nevins and Parker. We could call—"

"No, they'll arrest him on the spot."

"Maybe that's a good thing. He'll be safe from the drug cartel."

"But not from corrupt police. I don't trust them, Aiden. Any of them."

Aiden studied her. "There might be another way."

"What?"

"I could have Zack track the GPS on your brother's phone."

"Would you?"

"Yes, but if we locate him, we call Nate. No one goes after Danny. You do not leave this apartment, hear me?"

She nodded.

"Say it."

"I will not leave this apartment, unless I'm with you."

"Good. I'll make the call."

*She was running, trying to get to her brother; to help him, save him.*

*But the forest was too dense, and she could barely see through the thick mass of trees ahead of her.*

*"Danny!" she called out.*

*Breathe. She had to breathe through the panic ricocheting through her body.*

*"Danny," she croaked.*

*"Nia!" his voice called back.*

*She pumped her fists, hopped a downed tree branch and headed toward the sound. Suddenly the forest opened up to a clearing that overlooked a valley, and she saw them: Danny and her stepfather.*

*"Leave him alone!" she cried.*

*Her stepfather grabbed Danny by the shoulders and threw him over the edge of the cliff.*

*"Nooooo!" she cried.*

"Nia!"

She gasped. Blinked open her eyes. A dream—it was only a dream.

"Hey, hey," Aiden said, tipping her chin.

She gazed into his warm blue eyes.

"Carter tracked your brother's cell signal," Aiden said.

"He's okay?"

"I've called it in to Nate. They're setting up a search team."

She glanced at her surroundings, remembering how she'd ended up here, in Quinn's private apartment. Although Aiden had called the IT tech the previous night to track Danny, her brother's phone had been turned off and they couldn't get a signal until it went back on. She'd spent the better part of the night fidgeting with tension, fearing that he'd been killed. But it looked as if now they had a lead on his whereabouts, because he'd turned his phone back on.

Aiden said Danny had probably turned off the phone because he didn't want to be found by his pursuers. Sometime in the middle of the night Aiden finally convinced Nia to rest, and promised to wake her if they found her brother.

"What time is it?" she said, sitting up.

"Six-thirty. Did you get any sleep?" he asked, brushing a strand of hair off her face.

His touch felt so gentle and calming. "I think so. When is the team heading out?"

"Shortly."

"Are you joining them?" she asked.

"I'll stay here. I don't want to risk anything happening to you again."

"I'd rather you help find Danny, unless they're only sending police into the mountains."

"You want me to go?"

She nodded. "Even though you and Danny don't get along, he might come out of hiding because he knows that you and I are friends. You should go, and tell him I sent you."

"I don't know, Nia. If something were to happen to you while I'm gone—"

"I won't leave the apartment. You said yourself that this place is like Fort Knox. I'll be safe."

He pursed his lips, considering. She thought he might refuse her request, but then something shifted in his expression. "Okay, if that's what you want. I need to check in with the day staff first. Then I'll call Nate."

"Thank you so much." She hugged him, wishing she could hold on to this man forever.

That was when she realized her feelings had gotten away from her, that she was developing an unhealthy romantic attachment to Aiden.

"Sorry." She broke the embrace.

"Don't be." He offered a half smile. "Zack will work from the apartment today so you're not alone." He glanced at the dining room table where the IT tech sat, engrossed in his laptop. Zack Carter was in his early thirties with flyaway reddish-brown hair, hipster glasses and a two-day growth of beard. He mostly kept to himself but was always friendly when Nia asked him questions about the resort's computer system.

"Zack?" Aiden said.

"Yeah, boss?"

"You work from here and keep an eye on Nia. No one comes in or leaves. You got me?"

"Yes, sir. What about room service, sir?"

"I'll have my sister bring something by for breakfast and lunch. Do not answer the door for anyone but her. That's an order."

"I understand," Zack said.

Aiden turned back to Nia. "I'm only doing this because I have your word you'll stay put. I'll have Bree swing by with a change of clothes, as well."

"Thank you."

He stood and she grabbed his hand. "And thank you for helping find my brother."

Aiden and the team headed in the direction of the GPS signal, straight up a trail on the south end of Echo Mountain. What was Nia's brother doing out here, anyway? It didn't make any sense.

Today's team was mostly law enforcement: Deputy Nate Walsh; Harvey, the resort's former security officer and a retired cop; and a new guy to Echo Mountain SAR, Spike Duggins. Spike was a community service officer for Wallace Falls PD and was hoping to become a police officer someday.

Nate had tried to get Aiden to stay back, especially considering his bad knee, but Aiden had made a promise to Nia and told Nate it was a losing argument.

They'd hiked about two hours into the national forest and were approaching Talus Ridge when Nate got a call from base.

"This is Deputy Walsh, over."

"We're rerouting a call from the resort, over," the field command coordinator said.

The resort? Aiden gripped the strap on his backpack. Nia.

"This is Zack Carter. The GPS signal is moving."

"In which direction, over?" Nate said.

"I'm forwarding the signal to you so you can follow it."

"Roger that." Nate studied his phone.

Aiden wanted to ask if Nia was okay, if she'd eaten anything and if she was resting her ankle instead of pacing on it. But he had to stay focused, which wasn't easy after last night's intimacy, the conversation about forgiveness and the way she'd touched his cheek.

"I've got a location," Nate said to his team. "But I want to clarify that if he's armed, you guys stay behind me." He looked at Spike. "All of you. Got me?"

"I brought a firearm," Spike said.

"And if you discharge that firearm I will not put in a good word for you with Echo Mountain PD or the sheriff's department. This is a search-and-rescue mission, not a *Dirty Harry* movie." Nate took a step closer to the kid. "Are you reading me?"

"Loud and clear, sir."

"Good."

Harvey bit back a smile.

They continued hiking for twenty minutes and took a sharp turn back down. "Where is he going?" Nate muttered.

"At least we know he's okay," Harvey offered, glancing at Aiden. Harvey knew Nia pretty well and no doubt worried if they found her brother's dead body, she'd be devastated.

They hiked another half mile in silence. Suddenly Spike pointed to a trail below. "Check it out, sir."

The four men glanced over the edge of the trail. A motionless body lay a few hundred feet below. But was it Danny?

"Let's set up," Nate said. "Aiden and I will head down

with the litter. Harvey and Spike, keep an eye out, and help lift him up once he's secure."

"And if I see someone?" Spike said.

Nate narrowed his eyes at him.

"Do not discharge my firearm," Spike said.

Nate glanced at Aiden. "Ready?"

"Yep."

The men secured their lines to a sturdy tree and lowered themselves to the area below. It wasn't going to be easy securing the victim to the litter, considering the uneven ground.

Aiden touched down first, adjusting his footing against the damp earth. Nate landed on the other side of the body.

"Nia's going to be crushed," Aiden said.

"Let's turn him over."

Nate knelt and slowly turned over the body. It wasn't Danny. Aiden breathed a sigh of relief.

"Looks like a gunshot wound to the chest." Nate pressed his fingers against the man's throat, glanced up at Aiden and shook his head.

Nate radioed in. "This is Deputy Nate Walsh, over."

"Go ahead, over."

"This is now a recovery mission—male, Caucasian, forties with brown hair and a beard."

"Copy that, over."

Nate clipped the radio onto his belt and they got started securing the deceased onto the litter.

Nate's phone vibrated with a text. He glanced at it and frowned.

"What's wrong?" Aiden questioned.

"Danny's phone signal. It's moving again."

This motivated the team to pick up the pace. They set up a pulley system and carefully raised the body to the trail above. Aiden and Nate pulled themselves back up and the team headed to base camp.

"Harvey and I can follow the signal," Aiden said, figuring Nate had to stay with the deceased.

"No need. We're headed in that direction anyway."

"He's headed back down?" Aiden said.

"Looks like it," Nate said.

Which meant what? Danny had killed this man and fled the area?

"He looks like he's been dead for a few days," Nate offered, as if he knew where Aiden's brain was headed. "We'll follow the signal as long as it leads us in the direction of base camp."

It wasn't easy bringing a body down the trail, so the men took turns carrying the litter. They were within half a mile of the command post when Nate put up his hand. "The signal is headed this way." He glanced at Aiden then at Spike. "Spike, I'm putting you in charge of the body. You and Harvey take him to Command. Have them call the ME's office for pickup, and stay with the deceased until you sign it over."

Spike straightened. "Yes, sir."

"Aiden and I will follow the signal."

They split up, Aiden appreciating that Nate allowed him to continue the search for Danny.

"Thanks for letting me tag along," Aiden said.

"Don't make me regret it."

"Meaning what?"

"Don't go ballistic on me when we find him."

"Why would I do that?"

"Because you're angry with him for putting his sister's life in danger." Nate glanced back at Aiden. "The signal stopped moving. It looks close to your sister's cottage."

Aiden wouldn't lose it; he couldn't lose it. Nate was trusting him to maintain control, and Aiden would be useless if fear and worry distracted him from their mission: find Danny and bring him in.

"May I call my sister to make sure she's okay?" Aiden asked.

"Of course."

Aiden calmly pulled out his phone and called Bree.

"Hello, dear brother."

"Where are you?" he asked.

"Where are you?" she teased.

"Please, Bree, tell me where you are."

"On my way to deliver food to Nia. Why?"

"Where, *exactly*, are you?"

"About ten feet, four inches away from the coffee station in the lobby, which is twenty feet, seventeen inches from the front desk and—"

"Thank you for taking care of Nia," he interrupted. "Stay with her. Do not go back to your cottage until I say it's okay."

"Look, Mr. Bossy Pants—"

"Bree, please…" He took a breath. "Can you do this for me?"

She must have heard something in his voice. "Okay, sure."

"I'll check in later."

He ended the phone call, afraid he'd snap at his sister if she kept needling him. He didn't want to explain what was going on, not until they had the situation under control.

"You and your sister enjoy that whole sparring thing?" Nate said.

"You'd think so, wouldn't you?"

"I'm glad she's safe."

"I'm surprised you chose me to come with you instead of Spike or Harvey."

"I have a sister. I'd want to be there if I thought she was in trouble."

They continued in the direction of the cottage and Aiden wondered what they'd find. Was Danny hanging around the cottage because he thought Nia was there? Why couldn't he leave her alone?

Nate eyed his phone. "The signal is coming from the back of the house on the west side. I'm going to call it in."

"Shouldn't we—"

"No, we shouldn't. With any luck, sheriff's deputies will beat us there." Nate pulled his radio off his belt. "Dispatch, this is Deputy Walsh. I need backup at Echo Mountain Resort, cottage on the north end of the property, behind the lodge. We suspect Danny Sharpe is hiding out there, over."

"Help is on the way, over."

Nate and Aiden approached the trailhead leading to the resort. "We'll see if we can locate him, but keep out of sight," Nate ordered.

He motioned them off trail. Using the trees as cover, they made their way directly behind Bree's cottage.

"I don't see anyone," Aiden said. "Are you still getting a signal?"

"Yep, by the cottage. Hasn't moved since we called it in."

The blare of the resort's alarm echoed across the property.

"Did you have a drill scheduled?" Nate asked.

"Not that I know of." Although Aiden's head had been elsewhere these past few days, he wouldn't have forgotten a full resort evacuation. Panic coursed through him. What if this was a way to get Nia out in the open?

"Nia." Aiden took off running.

# ELEVEN

Aiden sprinted across the lawn, slowing down only when he approached guests who were evacuating the building. He didn't want them to be freaked out by a crazy man bolting toward them.

"Excuse me," he repeated a few times as he slipped between guests gathering outside. They looked understandably distressed.

*Join the club.*

Nia had promised to stay in the apartment, but even Aiden couldn't fault her for leaving the building if she thought it had caught fire, which it obviously hadn't. At least, it didn't look like it from this vantage point.

He whipped open the door to the north end of the building and rushed to Quinn's apartment. With a closed fist he pounded on the door.

"Nia!" But she wouldn't be able to hear him over the high-pitched squeal of the alarm. He realized he had his master key, so he stuck it in the lock and opened the door. "Nia!"

He rushed through the main living area and then checked the two bedrooms. The place was empty. No Zack, no Bree and no Nia.

They couldn't have all been kidnapped during the fire-alarm chaos. It hadn't gone off more than a few minutes ago.

To calm himself, he assumed they had left the building, along with everyone else, for their own safety. He had to keep thinking that way or he'd go nuts.

He passed through the lobby to do a quick check on employees. Tripp was still manning the front desk.

"What triggered the alarm?" Aiden shouted.

"Not sure!"

The wail of sirens echoed out front.

"Lock up and help the fire crew!" Aiden ordered the twentysomething desk clerk.

Tripp nodded and rushed outside. Aiden made sure the registers and computers were locked and took off in search of Nia. He wanted to help the fire department locate the source of the alarm but needed to find Nia more.

As he made his way through to the other end of the lobby, he noticed a small figure huddled in the corner—a child.

He crouched down beside a little blond boy, who couldn't have been more than seven years old. The child looked up at Aiden with tears in his eyes, and Aiden offered his hand. Surprisingly, the boy took it. Aiden picked him up and carried him outside.

"Where's your mom?" Aiden asked.

"I dunno."

"Bobby!" a woman cried, running over to them. "I thought he was at the pool with his sisters."

Aiden passed the boy to his mom.

"Bobby, my sweet boy," she said, squeezing her son in her arms.

"You didn't happen to see a young woman in her twenties with brown hair, hobbling around on crutches, did you?" Aiden asked.

"No, sorry," the mother said.

He turned to leave and she touched his arm.

"Thank you for saving my little boy."

With a nod, Aiden took off, deciding to do a perimeter check of the guests gathered out back. The resort wasn't anywhere near capacity, but there were still between fifty and sixty people that had evacuated the building.

Suddenly the alarm clicked off, blanketing the group in

silence. That was when he heard it, the sound of Nia's voice echoing across the property.

"We still need to wait for the fire department to give the A-OK," she said.

He could hear her but couldn't yet see her past the group ahead of him.

"It's important that we conduct these drills every few months to make sure the system is in working order," she continued. "When the lodge is at full capacity, we're responsible for the safety of more than five hundred guests."

"All clear!" Scott called from the building, motioning guests back inside.

As the group cleared, Aiden's eyes locked onto Nia's sweet face. She seemed happy to see him at first. Then her smile faded into a frown. She no doubt expected answers about her brother, and Aiden didn't have any.

A guest approached her with a question, forcing Nia to break eye contact with Aiden.

"That was freaky," Bree said, walking up to Aiden.

"The alarm?"

"Yeah, just random like that. Everyone was outside by the time Zack figured out there weren't any real fires."

"Where is Zack now?"

"Behind me."

Aiden spotted Zack leaning against a totem pole about ten feet away. A laptop bag strapped across his body, his eyes scanned the area, as if he was looking for danger.

"Don't rip into him," Bree said. "He did good."

"Yeah, I can see that."

Aiden appreciated that the IT tech was keeping a close watch on Nia.

A car pulled up behind Zack. Agents Nevins and Parker got out of the sedan and headed for Nia.

"Stay here," Aiden said and walked over to Nia.

Zack tried blocking the men, but Parker whipped Zack's

arm behind his back and pinned him to the totem pole. Nevins closed the distance between himself and Nia.

"Hello, Agent Nevins," Aiden said with as much charm as he could manage.

"Aiden, we thought you were on the rescue mission," Agent Nevins said.

"I was."

"Excuse me," Nia said to the guest. The fiftyish woman smiled and walked away. Nia looked at Aiden, expectant.

"Agent Parker, please release my IT tech," Aiden said. "He needs to get back to work."

"He assaulted me," Parker said.

"He was protecting Nia, which is what I'd asked him to do. In case you haven't heard, I can be a pretty nasty boss when my employees don't follow my orders."

"Let him go," Nevins said.

Parker released Zack, who glared at him.

"Zack, back to work," Aiden ordered.

Begrudgingly, Zack stormed off, muttering "bullies" under his breath.

"So, Danny?" Nia asked Aiden with hope in her eyes.

"They might have found him by now. I'm not sure," Aiden said.

"Might have found him?" Nevins said.

"We were tracking his cell signal. It led to the cottage." Aiden pointed. Two squad cars, lights flashing, pulled into the front driveway. "Looks like backup is here."

"You didn't find anything during your search in the mountains?" Nevins pushed.

"We recovered a body." He heard Nia gasp and he turned to her. "Not your brother."

She sighed and closed her eyes.

"Who was it?" Nevins asked.

"I didn't recognize him."

Agent Nevins glanced at the cottage, then back at Nia.

"We need to question Miss Sharpe about her encounter last night with Agent Brown."

"We tried contacting her immediately after it happened, but she seemed to have disappeared," Parker added.

"She was traumatized and needed to rest," Aiden said.

"She looks well rested now," Parker snapped.

"*She* is worried about her brother," Nia said calmly. She glanced at Aiden. "I'd like to see if he's at the cottage."

"Let's give them a few minutes to secure the area, and then I'll check with Nate. Why don't you sit down." He motioned her to a wooden bench by the building. From there they could clearly keep an eye on the cottage.

"If I didn't know better, I'd think you were avoiding answering our questions, Miss Sharpe," Agent Nevins said.

"Pardon my candor, sir, but you don't know me at all. I have nothing to hide. Ask whatever you'd like."

The agents accompanied Nia and Aiden to the bench.

"What did Agent Brown say to you last night?" Nevins said.

"He was asking about Danny, where he kept the two hundred thousand dollars, if we shared a bank account, stuff like that."

"Did Agent Brown say anything about his partner?" Nevins asked.

"No."

"Who shot Agent Brown?" Parker asked.

"I have no idea. Why don't you ask him?"

"We can't. He's dead."

Aiden studied the federal agent. "When?"

"A few hours ago. They couldn't stop the internal bleeding from his stomach wound."

"His stomach," Nia hushed. "I hit him in the stomach with my crutch."

"Hey, hey." Aiden grabbed her arm and gently sat her on the bench. "It's not your fault."

Aiden positioned himself next to her and placed a comforting hand on her shoulder. Instinct warned him to be careful about public displays of affection in front of the federal agents.

"Why was he trying to kidnap you?" Agent Parker asked.

"To lure my brother out of hiding."

"And he didn't say anything about what happened to Agent McIntyre?"

"She already said he didn't," Aiden snapped. His phone buzzed with a text. He grabbed it with his free hand. It was from Nate: Come to the cottage. Bring Nia.

That couldn't be good.

"What is it?" Agent Nevins said.

"They've secured the area around my sister's cottage."

Nia glanced into his eyes, hopeful.

"I don't know," Aiden said, reading her thoughts. "Nate didn't give me specifics, only that he wants us over there. Let's get a cart."

She nodded, seemingly distracted by the possibility of what she might find at the cottage. He led her to a nearby golf cart that staff routinely used to get from one end of the property to the other.

"We'll follow you," Agent Nevins said.

Aiden ignored him, solely focused on Nia. He helped her into the cart and she placed her crutches between them. He pulled away, casting a quick glance at Nia.

Touching her hand that rested on her thigh, he said, "It will be okay." He wasn't sure why he said it, or how he could make such a bold statement, but he sensed it would ease her tension.

She glanced at him and nodded her thanks.

Moments later, they pulled up to the cottage. Squad cars blocked the main driveway. Officer Carrington from Echo Mountain PD recognized Aiden and waved him through.

Aiden pulled up to the cottage and parked. Nia practically sprang out of the cart.

"Nia, wait."

But she was headed for the steps without her crutches before Aiden could catch up.

"Nia," Nate said from the side yard. "Over here."

She hesitated and looked at him. "My brother is…dead?"

"No, ma'am. We did not find him. Back here, please."

As Aiden and Nia followed Nate to the back of the house, Aiden spotted Agents Nevins and Parker being held back by Officer Carrington.

"We found a few things that might belong to your brother," Nate said. "A phone and this jacket." Nate hesitated beside the steps. A Detroit Lions jacket lay across the back porch, a smudge of red staining the front.

"Is that blood?" Nia asked.

"We're not sure," Nate said. "We'll have it tested after crime-scene photographs are taken. We also found this." Nate held up an evidence bag with a phone inside. "Is it your brother's?"

"It could be," she said. "I can't be sure."

Nate glanced at Aiden. "This is the signal we were tracking. Aiden, I was hoping you could let us inside to check out the cottage."

"Of course."

"We'll use the front entrance so we don't disturb this area." Nate motioned them to the front of the house.

"Do you think my brother is inside?" Nia asked.

"We don't know," Nate said.

"The alarm would have gone off," Aiden said.

"Unless he disarmed it somehow," Nate said.

"Not sure how he'd do that."

Agent Nevins called out to Aiden from the perimeter.

"Those are the second set of agents sent to retrieve Agents Brown and McIntyre," Aiden said.

Nate motioned to an officer standing beside a cruiser. The officer jogged over.

"Keep everyone away from the house until I give the

order. I'm not ready to involve the feds in a potential crime scene."

"Yes, sir."

Nate, Aiden and Nia went up the stairs to the front door. Aiden used the code to open the door and Nate went in first, motioning Aiden and Nia to stay behind him. Aiden disarmed the alarm.

"Alarm was set. He would have tripped it if he'd broken in," Aiden said.

"You two, please wait on the front porch while I search the house." Nate pulled his off-duty piece out of his holster and headed up the stairs.

"Why does he need a gun?" she said.

"Precaution."

"But my brother's not a violent man."

"Maybe not, but his business associates are extremely dangerous."

They stepped outside. Aiden spotted his sister and Scott marching toward them. In the background, the two federal agents were visibly upset that civilians had been allowed through, while they were being held back.

"Did someone break into my house?" Bree said.

"We don't know. There's some evidence on the back porch that police will want to photograph, so don't disturb that area."

"For how long?"

"Not sure yet," Aiden said. "Hey, where's the dog?"

"The dog has a name," Bree quipped.

"Sorry. Where's Fiona?" Aiden said.

"At the groomer getting beautiful."

"Okay, good," Aiden said.

The front door opened. "No sign of disturbance," Nate said. "I'll have the lab guys get over here as soon as possible, but until they're finished, I'm going to have to ask that you stay away from your house," Nate said to Bree.

"Can't I get some clothes and my toothbrush?"

"I'm afraid not. Hopefully they'll be done by tomorrow morning."

"Where am I going to sleep?"

"You can stay at Quinn's private apartment with Nia," Scott said, glancing at Aiden. "Right, boss?"

"That's an excellent idea."

Aiden got the women settled at Quinn's apartment and left Quinn a voice mail to keep him posted. Aiden knew Quinn would understand since not long ago he'd been in a similar situation trying to protect the woman he loved from danger. Now that woman was safe—and Quinn's fiancée.

Nia slept in the guest room, and Bree on the couch, while Aiden stayed up, keeping watch and trying to get some paperwork done. Scott relieved him at 3:00 a.m. and Aiden stretched out in the recliner, where he caught a few hours' sleep.

The next day things were quiet at the resort and seemingly back to normal. Aiden didn't trust the sudden calm. Although he successfully managed his responsibilities from Quinn's apartment, he was always on edge, waiting for the other shoe to drop.

His sister headed out to complete her grounds work for the day dressed in jeans and a T-shirt from the gift shop since she hadn't been allowed back into her cottage. Aiden guessed Scott would trail her as she made her rounds. She left Fiona behind with Nia for additional protection. Aiden glanced at the golden retriever, rolling on her back with a tennis ball wedged between her front paws. Protection? Hardly.

Nia was as efficient as ever, making calls, confirming plans and answering guest questions by phone. It surprised him that she was managing things so well, considering the past five days.

"Our mud slide guests have all been allowed back into their homes, which is good since there's a SAR meeting scheduled for 7:00 p.m. in the barn. We've got a Merry

Berry Farm tour booked for this afternoon and a family movie scheduled in the lobby at seven."

He glanced at her across the dining room table, studying a folder. "You are remarkable."

"I don't know about that."

"With everything that's going on, you're still able to focus. Wish I could say the same about myself."

"It's all about compartmentalizing things. I imagine putting them in a box and locking them away until I have time to deal with whatever the issue is. This thing with Danny is frightening, sure, but it can't stop us from providing excellent service to our guests. I mean, it's all about making people happy while on vacation, right?"

"I suppose that's one way of looking at it." He leaned back in his chair.

"And another way is…?"

"It's a job, a way to earn an income."

"That's awfully cynical, even for you."

"Why are you so determined to see the good in me?"

"Why are you so determined to only see the bad?" She winked.

"This is a losing argument."

"Who's arguing?"

A knock sounded at the door and Fiona barked.

"Good girl," Aiden said and went to check the peephole. It was Nate.

Aiden swung open the door. "Good morning. Come on in."

"Thanks." Nate went to the dining area. "You'd better sit down."

"That doesn't sound good." Aiden joined Nia at the table.

"I've got news. First, the fire alarm was intentionally pulled. I was with Scott this morning going through the surveillance feed."

"Who was it?" Aiden said.

"We couldn't identify him. Or her. The perpetrator knew where the cameras were pointed."

"So he's an employee?"

"Or she," Nia offered.

"Could be," Nate said. "There's more. The man we found yesterday in the mountains?"

Aiden automatically reached for Nia's hand. He wasn't sure why.

"He was identified as Agent Mark McIntyre."

"Oh no. And my brother is responsible?" Nia pulled her hand from Aiden's and stood, taking a few steps away.

"Hey," Aiden said. "Crutches."

She waved him off. "I'm fine. But I'm frustrated and ashamed."

"What are you talking about?" Aiden went to her. "None of this is your fault."

"Isn't it? If only I could have…"

"What? You can't force someone to make better choices in life."

"But why did he have to bring all this here?"

"That's a good question," Nate said. "You think he came to say goodbye? Like he was falling off the grid and wanted to see his sister one last time?"

"I'd like to think he cared that much about me, but it's more likely he came here because he needed money."

A sudden knock at the door set the dog on another round of barks.

"It's okay, girl," Aiden said. He glanced into Nia's eyes. "It will be okay."

He thought she nodded.

The knocking continued. "Aiden? Bree?" Scott called.

Aiden opened the door and Scott rushed into the apartment, searching the living room. "She's here, right? Bree's here?" Scott's voice cracked.

"She's not back yet," Aiden said. "Scott, what's going on?"

"I lost her, Aiden. I was following her and got distracted by a suspicious-looking pickup, and when I turned around, she was gone."

# TWELVE

"When did you see her last?" Aiden asked.

"South end of the property behind the barn. She's not answering her phone or text messages. She's in trouble. I know she's in trouble. She always answers my text messages."

"Take a breath," Aiden said. Scott had launched into full-blown panic mode, and Aiden needed to pull him back from the edge. "She wanders into the forest sometimes to get ideas from the wildflowers. Besides, she's very capable of taking care of herself."

Although he said the words to calm Scott down, Aiden was also worried. It wasn't like her not to answer her cell phone.

"Can the police help?" Nia asked Nate.

"She hasn't been gone long enough for them to do anything official," Scott answered before Nate could respond. "But I feel like every minute counts."

"We'll call some friends to help search for her." Nia pulled out her phone.

"Start with Harvey and Will," Aiden said. "Harvey will take over for Scott here at the resort, and Will can join us in the search. Get in touch with Zack and have him ping her cell phone to get a lock on her location."

"I'm on it," Nia said.

"Why do you think she's in trouble?" Nate questioned Scott.

"Gut instinct." Scott paced to the sliding door, pumping his fists with nervous energy.

Scott and Bree had developed a deep and serious relationship after Bree had found him wounded on a trail. Bree had essentially saved Scott's life, and Aiden knew they were connected in a profound way. They'd fallen in love.

"Harvey's on his way," Nia said.

"Good." Aiden stepped in front of Scott as he paced. "We need to stay calm."

"I know, I know," Scott said.

"I can keep watch over Nia," Nate offered.

Aiden glanced at Nia. She nodded. "Go. Go find your sister."

Her phone beeped and she glanced at it. "It's a text from Will. He's on his way."

"Tell him to meet us at the barn," Aiden said.

She grabbed his hand. As he gazed into her eyes, his heart swelled at what he saw there. True caring. Maybe even…love?

"Be careful," she said.

"I promise." He pressed a gentle kiss against her cheek, turned quickly and led Scott out of the apartment.

Half an hour later Aiden was having a hard time keeping it together. They'd found Bree's resort baseball cap on the edge of a trail leading up into the mountains. What he'd hoped was a misunderstanding was turning out to be more serious. That was when they picked up official gear, including a litter, just in case.

As Aiden, Scott and Will hiked the trails leading from the barn into the national forest, the pit in Aiden's stomach grew bigger.

Scott hadn't said much of anything in the past half hour. The expression on his face made it hard for Aiden to look at him. Scott seemed lost, maybe even resigned to accept the worst-possible scenario.

"Aiden!" a man called from behind them.

They hesitated as Dr. Spencer jogged up the trail. "Figured you could use a fourth. I picked up a radio at the barn."

"Thanks, Doc," Aiden said.

"Spence," he corrected him and turned to Will. "We haven't met. Kyle Spencer."

"Will Rankin."

The men continued up the trail. Scott had nodded his greeting to the doc but still hadn't spoken.

"Rankin, as in the adorable Rankin girls?" Spence teased Will.

"Yeah, those would be the ones." Will shook his head. "Adorable and charming. I'm in deep trouble."

Spence smiled.

A few minutes later they approached a fork in the trail.

"Let's split up," Aiden said. "Spence and Will, go left. Scott and I will go right. Use the radios to stay in touch."

Aiden and Scott hiked about ten minutes when Scott finally spoke. "This is a waste of time."

"Do you have a better idea?"

"Yeah. Fire me."

"Not likely."

"Why not? If I can't protect the one thing I care about the most, then I'm certainly not qualified to be your security manager."

Aiden knew Scott was a strong and confident man, but the thought of losing the woman he loved was ripping his confidence to shreds.

It would surely rip Aiden's confidence, and much more, to shreds if anything happened to Nia.

Reality slammed into Aiden's chest. He was falling in love with Nia. *Falling? You're already there, buddy.*

He shoved the thought aside, needing to focus on his sister.

"We're going to find her and she'll be okay." Aiden hesitated. "I won't accept any other scenario."

"But after everything she's been through," Scott said.

"At least the trauma from dating her ex inspired her to become a black belt."

Scott actually cracked a slight smile. "Yeah, she told me she knew karate early on in our relationship."

"Trying to scare you away, huh?"

"More like she was letting me know she could protect me."

"Then believe in Bree and her ability to take care of herself."

"Why would anyone bring her up here? And why Bree? She's got nothing to do with all this."

Aiden shook his head. He figured Scott needed to vent but didn't really expect an answer.

"Aiden, we've found…at the…over," Will said through the radio.

Aiden yanked it off his belt and hesitated on the trail. "Repeat, over."

"…past the…is the…"

"Will? Repeat, over."

There was no response.

"Aiden, now!" Spence's voice carried through the radio.

Without a second's hesitation, Aiden and Scott took off in the direction of their other team members. They'd obviously found something, or maybe even found Bree.

*Please, God, Bree's already been through so much.*

Asking for God's help didn't feel uncomfortable or wrong this time. He wondered if Nia's faith was rubbing off on him.

They jogged back to the fork in the trail and Scott slipped as he made a turn. Aiden grabbed his jacket and yanked him back from the edge.

Scott nodded his thanks and they kept moving.

A woman's scream echoed up the trail. Scott ran faster, Aiden struggling to keep up. Minutes later, Aiden spotted Spence on his knees, looking over the edge of the trail.

"Doc!" Scott shouted. "Doc, what is it?"

"Breanna. Down there."

Scott skidded to a stop and dropped to his knees. "Bree! Bree, are you okay?"

"No, I'm not okay. I'm fuming angry! Throw me a rope, something to haul me up."

Scott shucked his backpack and pulled out a rope.

Relieved that his sister was okay, Aiden realized Will was missing.

"Spence, where's Will?" Aiden said.

"He went after the guy."

"What guy?" Aiden tensed.

"I don't know. Some guy who assaulted Bree on the trail."

"Assaulted her?" Scott froze.

Spence grabbed the rope. "I'm sorry—bad choice of words. We don't know what happened. Let's get her up here so we can find out the details."

With a nod, Scott started to wrap the rope around his body. "I'll go get her."

"Wait," Aiden said. "Bree, you need Scott to come down there and get you?"

"No! There's not enough room for both of us. Make a loop on the end of the rope and pull me up."

Aiden nodded at Spence. "Can you guys handle this? I need to find Will."

"Yeah, go," Spence said.

Aiden took off, realizing he no longer needed to be Bree's number one champion and protector. She had Scott now, a man so deeply in love with her he couldn't even speak when he thought her life was in danger.

Aiden would be the same way if anything happened to Nia.

He picked up his pace, wishing Will hadn't put himself in danger this way, but the guy had a big heart and considered himself something of a protector, as well. That probably had something to do with raising two little girls.

Aiden approached a switchback and heard what sounded like grunting, and then a gun went off.

"No," Aiden groaned. Claire and Marissa Rankin had

lost their mom to cancer. They couldn't lose their father, as well.

Aiden spun around the turn and spotted Will sprawled on the ground. Aiden scanned the area but he was alone.

"Will," he said, rushing to the man and pressing his fingers against his neck. His pulse was steady.

Aiden did a quick search of Will's body. No gunshot wounds.

"I didn't hit him that hard!" a man's voice cried.

Aiden glanced at the trail above him. Danny peered over the side, a gun in his hand.

"It's not my fault!" Danny cried.

"It's okay. I believe you," Aiden said.

"You don't. I know you don't!"

"I have to believe you, Danny. I'm your sister's friend and she cares about you very much."

"Where is she? Is she here?" Danny whipped his head from side to side.

Something wasn't right. The guy looked...crazed.

"She's back at the resort. I'm keeping her safe for you, Danny. Why don't you come back with me and talk to her."

"No!" He pointed a gun at Aiden. "It's a trick. They're all trying to trick me to get the money."

"I'm not trying to trick you." Aiden put up his hands in a submissive gesture. "I'm trying to help my friend Nia. She's so worried—"

"She doesn't have to worry because I'm going to find her and save her!" He spun around and disappeared from view.

"Danny!"

But he was gone. Aiden's priority had to be Will, then getting word back to the resort that Danny could be coming after his sister. Aiden yanked the radio off his belt and found himself praying it would work properly. "Spence, this is Aiden, over."

Aiden glanced at Will's hand. One or both of his girls had drawn flowers on his palm. Aiden looked away.

"Spence, this is Aiden, over," he tried again.

"We got her," Spence said. "Your sister's safe, over."

"Good. I need your help. Will's hurt. About five hundred feet north of our position past the switchback, over."

"On my way, over."

Aiden clipped the radio to his belt and leaned back to see if he could spot Danny. If Aiden didn't know any better, he'd think the guy was high on something. Yet he seemed genuinely worried about Nia.

But why hurt Bree? Did he accidentally hurt her? And why bring her up here?

Will moaned, his eyes cracking open and then closing.

"Hey, welcome back," Aiden said.

Will blinked again and this time his eyes stayed open, although they didn't look as if they were totally focused. "Where's Claire?" Anxious, Will tried to sit up.

"Hey, hey, your girls aren't here, Will. We were on a search mission to find Bree, remember?"

"The girls are okay?"

"They're fine."

Will nodded and closed his eyes.

"Will?"

Will opened his eyes and looked at Aiden in question.

"Do you know who I am?" Aiden asked.

"Aiden McBride."

"Where were you born?"

"San Francisco."

"What year is it?"

"It's 2015."

"Good. You're okay, buddy." Aiden patted Will's jacket.

"Uh...not really. I'm gonna get a lecture from Megan about being hurt on a SAR mission."

Aiden sucked in his breath. Megan was Will's dead wife.

"I'm sure it will be fine," Aiden said, hoping this was a temporary lapse in Will's memory.

Because Aiden knew Nia would never forgive herself if

the single father couldn't care for his children because of an injury sustained at the hands of her brother.

They tried carrying Will down the trail but he wouldn't have it. He grew belligerent, another sign of brain trauma, and Spence decided to be extra patient and kind.

Aiden called Nia and told her to stay put until he returned from taking Bree and Will to the hospital to get checked out.

Bree seemed physically fine, except for a few scratches on her cheek. But man, she was fired up.

"I can't believe I fell for that guy's act, but he looked so desperate."

"Kind of like I did, huh?" Scott said.

"This is not your fault," Bree said.

"Sure it is. I never should have let you out of my sight."

"Oh really? And you're going to glue yourself to my side from now on?"

"If I have to."

"I'm *so* not into controlling men. You know that."

"I'm being protective, not controlling."

"Semantics."

As they bantered back and forth, Aiden kept an eye on Will. He seemed to be able to navigate the trail but had grown quiet, as if he was worried about disappointing his wife.

The doc said Will's injuries were minor, but he'd suffered a head injury that required a CT scan.

"And Danny was so upset about Nia," Bree said, glancing at Aiden.

"What did he say, specifically?" Aiden asked.

"That they were after her, too. He said she was hiding up by Crystal Point, and I followed him because I thought if she was really up there and you didn't know where she was, you'd be a wreck. Then halfway up the trail he spun around and started hammering me with questions about Nia, who her friends were, where she was staying, and I'm thinking, if he's really got her hidden, then why doesn't he just ask her? I knew he was lying, so I fired off a heel-palm strike and took off."

"Did he push you off the trail?" Aiden asked.

"No, I actually climbed down to hide."

"Smart girl," Scott said.

"Not so smart or I would have been able to pull myself up without your help."

"Hey, you're the one who taught me to accept help, sweetheart. Maybe you should take your own advice?" Scott offered.

Bree shrugged.

They were almost at the resort. They couldn't get there fast enough for Aiden. He wanted to get to Nia, hug her, tell her that her brother was alive and everything was going to be fine, but he needed to stay with Will and Bree, make sure they were okay. Besides, Nia was safe under the watchful eye of Deputy Nate Walsh.

"Did Danny say anything that would indicate where he was going?" Aiden asked Bree.

"Nope."

"What about you, Will?" Scott said. "You get anything out of the guy before he took off?"

Will's eyebrows furrowed. "I…I don't remember."

Bree and Scott shared a look of concern.

"A little fogginess is to be expected after a head injury," Spence offered with a reassuring smile.

"Yeah," Will said.

But he didn't look convinced. He seemed lost and confused. The sooner they got him to the hospital, the better.

Although Aiden had asked her to stay at the resort, Nia knew she'd be safe in a hospital full of people with Nate as her police escort. She needed to be there for her friends Bree and Will.

As Nate accompanied her to the hospital emergency

room entrance, he scanned the surrounding area with precision.

"Did he tell you the extent of their injuries?" Nate asked.

"No, only that they weren't serious."

They entered the ER and asked the receptionist about Bree and Will. She suggested they take a seat in the waiting room.

A few minutes later, Aiden came out of the examining area. He looked pale, and worry lines creased his forehead.

She stood and went to him. "Aiden?"

He snapped his attention to her. He looked angry, not at all happy to see her.

"What are you doing here?" He gently took her by the arm and led her back to the lounge.

"I was worried about my friends and you."

"I told you they weren't seriously hurt. Didn't you believe me?"

"Of course I did, but I needed to be here." She studied his expression. "What's going on?"

He motioned her to sit near Nate so he could hear, as well.

"Good news, bad news," he started. "Bree is fine. Minor scratches, bruises, that sort of thing. Also, Danny is alive."

Relief washed over her. "He's not hurt or wounded or anything?"

"It didn't look like it."

"You saw him?"

"I did."

"Why didn't he come down with you?"

"He seemed a little off, Nia. Paranoid, borderline psychotic."

"No, that's not Danny. He's laid-back to a fault."

"Well, he didn't seem like himself, then."

"Was he on something?" Nate interjected.

Nia studied Aiden as he answered. "Possibly."

"Wait—how did you run into Danny?" Nia said.

"He was up in the mountains. He—" Aiden paused "—he lured Bree up a trail."

"He kidnapped Bree?"

"He didn't kidnap her, exactly. She went willingly. She was worried because he was ranting about you being in danger. The sheriff's office and feds are working together to send a team into the mountains to find him."

"That's the bad news, isn't it?" Nia said.

"Actually, there's one more thing." Aiden took her hand in his and squeezed. "Will suffered a head injury after getting into a scuffle with your brother. Will's a little confused and they don't know how long it will take for the swelling to go down and things to get back to normal."

"Confused. You mean he doesn't remember who he is? Like when Scott had amnesia?"

"No, it's not like that. Will thinks Megan is still alive."

"Oh, Aiden." A ball of emotion lodged in her throat.

Aiden pulled her against his chest and stroked her back in such a soothing way. Nia felt responsible and devastated. Poor Will would have to relive the grief of losing his wife.

Because of Danny.

"This is so wrong," Nia said.

"Let's stay positive. Scott recovered, and he suffered a more severe head injury." He broke the embrace and looked into her eyes. "It will be okay."

"What are they doing here?" Nate said.

Agents Nevins and Parker marched across the lobby.

"Aiden McBride," Agent Nevins said. "We need you to come with us."

# THIRTEEN

"Wait—what? Why?" Nia said, getting up and effectively blocking them from speaking to Aiden.

"Hindering an investigation, for starters," Agent Nevins said. "And we need to ask some questions about questionable business practices at the resort."

"I don't understand." Nia glanced at Aiden. He hadn't uttered a word and she wondered if he was drifting into some kind of posttraumatic place, or if he was stunned by this development.

"Mr. McBride?" Agent Parker motioned with his hand for Aiden to join them.

Aiden stood in a robotic fashion.

"Hang on," Nia said. "His sister is in the hospital. He needs to stay and make sure she's okay."

"It's our understanding Scott Becket is with her."

"Are you arresting him?" Nate finally said, as if he'd been in too much shock to speak up before.

"Not yet." Parker eyed Aiden.

Nia noticed Aiden clench his jaw as if he struggled to remain in control. Ah, that was it. They wanted him to lose control so they could lock him up for assaulting federal officers. Aiden would be out of the way if he was sitting in jail, and they could focus their attention on Nia without Aiden's interference.

Once again, someone she cared about was being manipulated in order to get to me. She simply wouldn't have it.

Agent Parker took a step toward Aiden.

Nia got between them. "Let's go, Aiden."

"Ma'am, we can have you both arrested," Parker threatened.

"For what? Coming in for an interview? Believe it o not, we want to solve my brother's case just as much, if no more, than you do, Agent Parker. We will follow you to the office. Where are you parked?"

Aiden glanced at her. "Nia, no."

"Yes. You've always said you function better when I'n around, so let's get this over with."

The feds were smarter than Aiden had given them credi for. They'd figured out the way to Nia was through Aider because she'd do whatever was necessary to support him.

Even walk into a federal office to be interrogated.

Well, not exactly an FBI office, since the closest one was nearly two hours away in Seattle. But they'd convinced Chie Washburn of Echo Mountain PD to loan them space for the interrogation into the bogus accusations.

Nia demanded the feds let Aiden speak to his sister before he left the hospital, which got Bree even more workec up. But the fact that the agents had agreed to Nia's demanc proved they were manipulating the situation. They wantec her to think she had power, when, in fact, neither Nia nor Aiden had any power over what was about to happen. Ther again, they had the power of choosing their words very carefully.

"Questionable business practices. That's nonsense," Nia said in a soft voice as they waited in the conference room for the agents to return.

She'd been firm and demanding with the agents, yet when alone with Aiden she let her guard down. She trustec him.

And now he'd led her here, into the lion's den.

Aiden paced to the window overlooking the parking lot. "You shouldn't have come with me, Nia."

"Why? We both know that's what they wanted."

He snapped around and studied her.

"Yeah, I figured it out. They think I'm somehow connected to my brother's business, or I know something, or I can get them something. Whatever. It's about time I dealt with this head-on instead of hiding behind you."

The door opened and Agent Nevins entered.

"Please, take a seat." He motioned Aiden to sit at the table across from Nia.

Instead, Aiden pulled a chair to her side. "So, how did I hinder your investigation?"

"Besides repeatedly denying us access to Miss Sharpe? You agreed to let us take a look at your computer system and locked us out. You also helped a suspect flee when you knew we needed to question him."

"What are you talking about?"

"You saw Danny Sharpe in the mountains and you let him go."

"I was tending to an injured man."

"You're not a doctor. You should have detained Danny Sharpe."

"I'm also not a cop. It's not my job to detain anybody."

"No, apparently not." Nevins studied a folder on the table in front of him. "It's your job to help your girlfriend's brother flee authorities."

As if she sensed Aiden's temper flaring, she placed her hand over his, resting on his thigh.

"I'm not his girlfriend," Nia said. "I'm his employee."

She repeated Aiden's words, spoken many times these past few days, but they suddenly sounded bitter and oh so wrong.

*You're much more than an employee, sweetheart. Much more.*

"As his employee, do you have access to the resort's operating funds?" Agent Nevins asked Nia.

"I do."

"And what about the Timberline fund?"

"I'm not familiar with that one."

Agent Nevins glanced at Aiden. "You want to explain it to her?"

How could he? Aiden had never heard of the fund before today.

"There's nothing to explain," Aiden said, growing worried that something was going on he didn't know about.

"Before you locked us out, we noticed the Timberline fund and tried figuring out from where the money originated." Nevins leaned back in his chair. "It's a mystery. Either of you want to share?"

Aiden squeezed Nia's hand, encouraging her to remain silent.

"We can't tell you anything if we know nothing about it," Aiden said.

"You're not a very good liar, Mr. McBride."

"I'm not lying."

"Then why were we abruptly denied access to resort accounts?"

"When did this happen?" Aiden asked.

"Early this morning."

Agent Parker joined them.

"I can look into it," Aiden said. "I'll ask my IT guy if there was a glitch in the system."

"Which still leaves the fact that you helped Danny Sharpe flee the area."

"No, sir, I did not. I have no motive for that. I want to protect Nia. Her brother's criminal associates pose a danger to Nia, and the resort, for that matter. Besides, I was in no position to bring him down with us."

"Why not?"

Aiden hesitated. "Because he was threatening me with a gun."

"Aiden," Nia hushed.

Aiden gently squeezed her hand.

Nevins leaned forward. "He has a gun?"

"Yes."

"What kind?"

"A pistol of some kind."

"Long barrel, short, what?"

"If I had to guess, I'd say a Glock."

The two agents shared a look.

"What did he say to you?" Nevins asked.

"That he was worried about Nia. That people were after her, too."

"Why would he think that?"

"Maybe because her apartment had been broken into and you guys won't leave her alone?"

"Smart guy, huh?" Parker yanked Aiden to his feet and flung him against the glass window. He pinned Aiden with steely-gray eyes and a forearm against his throat.

"Let him go!" Nia shouted.

"Parker, enough," Nevins said.

Aiden stared back at the furious agent, reading more than anger in his eyes.

"Maybe if you would have worked with us from the beginning, we wouldn't have lost two agents." Parker released Aiden and paced to the other side of the room, shoving his hands in his pockets.

"And McIntyre was missing his firearm," Parker continued. "Which is probably the gun Danny Sharpe is carrying. Two men are dead and he's our prime suspect."

"You don't know for sure that he shot them," Aiden said, surprised that he was defending Danny. "At least not until Forensics confirms time of death."

"It's okay." Nia reached up and touched Aiden's hand. "I'm ready to accept the fact my brother is responsible in one way or another for the agents' deaths."

The room fell silent. Aiden wanted desperately to change the facts, or at least whisk her out of here and take her someplace where no one, especially the aggressive agents, could bother her. He sat down next to her, wanting to stay as close as possible.

She glanced at Agent Nevins. "I'll do whatever I can to help you apprehend my brother."

Nia spent the next two hours giving the agents information about Danny. They said they needed to build a profile to anticipate what he might do next, where he'd go. The stakes had been raised beyond measure now that they suspected him of killing two federal agents. Even if the men had been corrupt, they didn't deserve to die.

Agent Nevins said Danny was the key to closing the corruption case on the two agents and putting a drug ring from the Midwest out of business. Agent Parker didn't speak much during the meeting, but he glared at Aiden a few times.

It was nearly nine o'clock and Nia realized neither she nor Aiden had eaten supper. She'd been too frantic about Bree's disappearance, and Aiden had gone from the search site to the hospital to the police station.

"May we continue tomorrow?" she said. "I'm exhausted and haven't eaten since lunch."

"We can bring something in," Nevins offered.

"No, thank you. We'll pick something up on the way back to the resort." She stood and so did the men.

"Thank you for your help, Miss Sharpe," Agent Nevins said. "We'll contact you tomorrow morning."

"How about afternoon?" Aiden said. "We've got some catching up to do at work."

Nevins ignored him and spoke directly to Nia. "I'll call around eleven and we can go from there."

Nia finally breathed a sigh of relief when they left the police station in Aiden's truck.

"You really didn't have to do that," he said.

"What?"

"Come with me."

"Sure I did."

"Are you...okay?"

"I am. Does that surprise you?"

"I guess a little. You seem different than when your brother first came to town."

"I've accepted that which I cannot change. Danny has chosen a dark path and I cannot pull him back."

"And it's not your fault?"

She glanced at him and felt her lips curl slightly in a melancholy smile. "It's not my fault."

"At least some good has come out of all this."

"What's that?"

"You giving up responsibility for your brother's choices."

"Yeah, it feels good to let go of guilt. You should give it a try."

"What do you mean?"

"Your friend Yates. He wouldn't want you to carry that around."

A few moments of silence filled the SUV.

"Got any thoughts about dinner?" he asked.

"I could really use a grilled cheese right about now."

"What, no Healthy Eats for you?"

"Actually, they have their own version of a grilled cheese with hormone-free cheese and gluten-free bread."

"Probably tastes like paste."

"Too bad they close at nine."

"Yeah, too bad," he said in a wry tone.

"It wouldn't hurt you to try something healthy once in a while."

"It might hurt my taste buds."

She smiled. "Thanks."

"For what?"

"For not being intense after everything we've been through today."

"Intense. You mean like how I usually am?"

"I never said that."

"You didn't have to."

"You want things done right. That's an admirable quality."

"Yeah, but my execution could use some work."

"It never bothered me." She glanced out the passenger window as they passed through town.

"Really?"

She looked at her boss. For some reason he looked like someone else right now, not the harsh-talking, hyperfocused manager of Echo Mountain Resort. He looked like a young, vulnerable man who needed affirmation.

"Really," she said. "I always suspected your harsh demeanor was hiding something else, like fear or worry. It's those blue eyes that gave you away."

"How so?"

"You can't have such kind blue eyes and be an ogre." She slapped her hand to her mouth.

"What?" he challenged.

"I'm sorry. I really said that, didn't I?"

"Called me an ogre? Yeah, you did."

"It's low blood sugar, exhaustion, worry about—"

"It's okay. I've been called worse," he teased. "Speaking of low blood sugar, want to pick up a pizza?"

She studied him. She'd insulted him by calling him an ogre to his face, and he wanted to pick up a pizza?

"No pizza?" he said.

"Um, sure. Pizza is fine."

"Good. Call it into Frankie's and we'll swing by."

They made it back to the resort around ten with pizza. Bree called with an update: she was fine, and Will was spending the night in the hospital for observation.

That threatened to ruin Nia's appetite, but Aiden said he hated eating alone and asked her to join him. They were on their second slice when they heard someone jiggle the apartment door handle.

Aiden jumped to his feet and grabbed a nearby lamp to use as a weapon.

"Get in the bedroom," he ordered.

"Aiden? Open up. It's Quinn."

Aiden rushed to open the door. Resort owner Quinn Donovan marched past Aiden. "What's the deal? My garage door wouldn't open and the key card didn't work."

He nodded at Nia. "Hey, Nia. You okay?"

"Yes, thank you."

Turning to Aiden, Quinn narrowed his eyes. "And you're using my fiancée's favorite lamp as a weapon because…?"

"Sorry, sorry." Aiden put it back on the table and plugged it in.

Quinn dropped his keys on the dining room table. "You want to tell me what's going on?"

"You got my messages, right?"

"About needing to use the apartment to protect Nia, yes."

"Well, today, Bree went missing, and when we found her, Will got into it with Nia's brother and was hospitalized. Then the feds brought me in for questioning."

Quinn studied Aiden. "Everything okay?"

"It's my fault," Nia said. "My brother's gotten himself into trouble and it followed him out here."

"But that doesn't explain the guest complaints we've been getting and the key cards not working."

"Guest complaints?" Aiden said.

"They've been leaving feedback on the website. I came back to check things out, determine what we need to do to fix this."

"I'm sorry." Aiden collapsed at the table as if his legs had given out on him.

"I appreciate that, Aiden, but I'm wondering if maybe you need to take a break from things around here."

Nia nearly fell off her chair. "You're firing him?"

"Of course not," Quinn said. "He's a great manager. But right now I think he needs to focus on keeping you safe. I'm also wondering how legitimate these feedback forms are."

"What do you mean?" Nia said. Aiden seemed too stunned to contribute to the conversation.

"May I?" Quinn motioned to the pizza.

"Please," Nia said.

Quinn grabbed a slice. "What I mean is, maybe this is another way to get at Aiden."

"Why would they want to get at Aiden?" Nia questioned.

"Because he's an obstacle. With Aiden out of the way, Danny's enemies can get to you, and if Aiden's distracted with work issues, like unhappy guests, well, you do the math." Quinn took a bite of pizza.

Nia studied Aiden. She certainly didn't want him sacrificing his job, even temporarily, for her. That was beyond a boss's responsibility.

"Maybe it really is time that I leave town," she suggested.

Aiden snapped his attention to her. "Absolutely not."

"If I'm gone, everyone's safe. There's no more danger to Bree or SAR members. If only I could find Danny and get him to disappear with me."

"Don't talk like that," Aiden snapped. "You're not going anywhere with that guy. He'll get you killed."

"Not intentionally," she said. It didn't change Aiden's hard expression. He was being pulled in so many different directions because of her.

If only she could put an end to all this.

"I'm trying to do the right thing," she said.

"Aren't we all?" Quinn offered. "So, why didn't my key card work?"

"We had to change the code so no one could breach the apartment," Aiden said.

Quinn sat down and continued eating his pizza.

"Where's Billie?" Nia asked, hoping to change the subject from her brother.

"She wanted to spend one more night in Seattle to scope out wedding venues." He eyed Nia. "No, we haven't set a date yet. That will depend on the venue. Was hoping you could help with things when the time comes?"

"I'd be honored," she said.

As they returned to the topic of her brother, and detailed everything that had happened in the past week, Nia sensed Aiden growing more distant. It was as if he felt ashamed about all that transpired on his watch, that he worried his boss would somehow think less of him for not managing things better. But the week's events were no more Aiden's fault than Nia's.

Although she'd accepted the fact her brother had possibly taken another man's life, she still worried about him. While the men continued their conversation, she said a silent prayer, asking God to help her brother.

"Tomorrow morning I'll have Zack investigate the feedback forms to determine if they were generated from our guests or by someone—or somewhere—else," Quinn offered.

"We had a fire alarm go off and a temporary power outage. Do you think that could be what caused guests to complain?"

"Doubt it," Quinn said. "Knowing Nia, she probably made it up to anyone who was inconvenienced with a free ice cream or something."

"I was trained well." She smiled at Aiden, but he wouldn't look at her. Had she upset him or was he—

A sudden bang on the outside sliding door made Nia yelp.

Quinn motioned them to stay back. He grabbed a baseball bat out of the front closet and stalked across the room to the sliding door.

# FOURTEEN

Aiden rushed to Nia and put his arm around her. They waited, the silence deafening.

Another bang echoed across the apartment, then tapping, as if someone was knocking to come in.

"Aiden?" Nia whispered.

He pulled her against his chest.

Quinn whipped aside the curtain, but Aiden couldn't see what was on the other side of the glass.

"Oh man," Quinn said, putting down the bat. "It's okay. Aiden, come help me."

Aiden went to his boss's side as Quinn slid open the door. They helped Zack Carter into the apartment. Aiden heard Nia gasp at the sight of a disheveled Zack: dirt and blood smudged his cheeks and hands, and his clothes were ripped.

"I came this way so they wouldn't find the apartment," Zack said.

Aiden and Quinn helped him to the sofa.

"I don't want to get blood on your couch."

"The couch can be replaced," Quinn said.

"What happened?" Aiden prompted.

"Some guys were hanging out by the barn. I went to investigate but stayed out of sight. They were talking about Danny Sharpe and finding Nia. But I knocked into something and they heard me. I ran. They came after me in their car. I couldn't see their faces. I disappeared up a trail and they didn't bother me after that. So I sneaked over Mr. Donovan's fence, hoping somebody would be here."

Aiden glanced at Nia. "Can you get some ice and a wash-cloth?"

"Sure." She went into the kitchen.

"You've gotta get her out of here," Zack said, panicked.

Aiden patted his shoulder. "We will, don't worry."

"If you want to leave now…" Quinn offered.

"That's what they're expecting," Aiden said. "They're probably waiting at the end of Resort Drive for my truck to pull out."

"You want to wait?" Quinn said. "Call the police?"

"Not exactly."

"You've got something in mind," Quinn said.

"We not only need to keep Nia safe, but we need to move this trouble away from the resort, as well."

"Agreed."

"Let's take control of this situation and intentionally lure them away from the resort. We'll make it obvious which car Nia is in and ask a few friends to run interference. Scott's with Bree, so I won't bother him. I'll call Nate and Harvey, and maybe even Chief Washburn. You guys are buddies, right?"

"We've gone on a fishing trip or two, yeah," Quinn said.

"Good. By the time Nia's tucked away safe and sound, the drug thugs will know she's off resort property, but they won't have a clue where we've taken her."

"I like the way you think," Quinn said.

*Good.* Aiden needed not only to protect Nia, but he also had a responsibility to the guests of Echo Mountain Resort.

"You'll stick close to Nia?" Quinn asked.

"I'd like to, yes."

"Excellent. I'll temporarily fill in for you as manager until things are resolved."

"But—"

"You need to do this, trust me. I've always blamed myself for not taking better care of Billie when criminals were after her. I kept getting distracted by work, by life, everything else. I want you to ignore everything else and focus on Nia. That's an order."

"Yes, sir. Thank you, sir."

"You know where you'll take her?"

"I have a pretty good idea, yes."

"Take me?" Nia said, coming into the room and tending to a cut on Zack's cheek. "Where are we going?"

"To my mom's farm."

She snapped her attention to him. "Aiden, no. We can't bring my troubles to your mom's home."

"She's on a shopping trip in Victoria with her lady friends. Won't be back until late tomorrow afternoon. The house has got a state-of-the-art security system we installed after Dad passed away. It'll serve the purpose—for one night, anyway."

"Let's get started on this distraction plan of yours," Quinn said.

Aiden called Nate and Harvey, while Quinn called Chief Washburn.

Ten minutes later, Aiden and Nia were ready to go. Once Nate, the chief and Harvey were in position, they'd text Aiden and he'd pull out of the resort with Nia in the passenger seat, easily seen.

The plan was simple: Nate would be waiting at the end of the driveway. Once Aiden knew they were being followed, Nate would pull over the car following Aiden for a traffic stop. Nia and Aiden would head into the Williamses' barn and switch cars with Chief Washburn, who would drive off in Aiden's car. After getting a good look at them, but not having anything to ticket them for, Nate would release the men, who would catch up to Aiden's car, driven by the chief. The chief and Harvey would lead the men in the opposite direction from the McBride farm.

Everyone agreed this plan should keep Nia safe for the next twelve hours or so.

"So, why did the feds bring you in for questioning?"

Quinn asked Aiden as they waited for the text messages indicating everyone was in position.

"They claimed I hindered their investigation, first by hiding Nia and then by locking them out of our network."

"No kidding?" Quinn said.

"I'm guilty of the first but have no idea what happened with their access. You told me to give them full access, and I did."

"That was me," Zack admitted, holding an ice bag against his cheek. He'd moved to a chair at the dining table, where he was nibbling pizza.

"You froze them out without my permission?" Aiden asked.

"They're jerks."

"That might be true, but you nearly got Aiden locked up," Quinn said.

"I couldn't help it. They were poking around in places where they shouldn't be, and I think they left a bug in the system, which I've been trying to eradicate for the last twenty-four hours."

"Why would they leave a bug in the system?" Quinn said.

"Like I said, they're jerks."

"I sense there's more to it," Aiden said. "Were you afraid they were going to find something they shouldn't?"

Zack glanced at Quinn, then back at his pizza.

"What is it, Zack?" Quinn said.

"They were digging around in your special files, Mr. Donovan."

"Special files?" Aiden asked. "This wouldn't have anything to do with something called Timberline, would it?"

"I didn't tell him," Zack defended.

"The feds told me," Aiden said. "They suspect money is being funneled into the Timberline mystery fund, and they don't know where it's coming from. Is there something I should know about?"

"It's personal." Quinn glanced at Aiden. "And perfectly legal."

Aiden and Nia shared a concerned look.

"Okay, fine," Quinn said. "It's a surprise for Billie. I've been fund-raising on the side to build a retreat center for the church, you know, for special events, Bible study, that sort of thing."

"That sounds lovely," Nia said. "But why don't you tell Billie?"

He shrugged. "I wasn't sure I could totally fund it. We're only about halfway there. It's kind of, well, part of her wedding present."

"That's so sweet," Nia said.

"My job was to keep an eye on it but not let anyone know about the fund," Zack said. "Fail."

"Hey, you didn't know the feds would go poking around," Quinn said.

Aiden's phone buzzed with a text. "It's Nate. Everyone's in position." He reached for Nia's hand. "You ready?"

"I am."

She seemed so confident that Aiden could take care of her, protect her from the faceless enemies waiting for them. Aiden wished he shared her confidence.

The plan worked seamlessly. Less than an hour later, Nia was settled at the McBride home, where she felt safe and at peace, at least for the time being.

They'd called Agents Nevins and Parker to let them know they were going into hiding but would check in tomorrow morning. Nia didn't want the agents to think she was trying to flee the state or anything.

Aiden asked Nia to relax in the living room while he made tea. It felt odd to be waited on by a man, but she was getting used to it. She was growing more comfortable with their role reversal: Aiden taking care of Nia, instead of the other way around.

Although she initially didn't want to stay here because of putting Aiden's mother in danger, Nia loved the McBride home. She'd attended their holiday open house two years in a row, a celebration where church and community members enjoyed delicious food, lively conversation and much-needed laughter. Every time she stood in this very living room she couldn't help but think how wonderful it must have been growing up in such a loving family.

She studied a line of framed photos on the mantel and noticed a picture of Aiden's father with his arm around his teenage son, dressed in his football uniform. It made her smile. Aiden's expression was typical for the age, aloof and disinterested. Yet she could sense his deep love for his father.

"I look like a dork, huh?" Aiden said, coming into the room carrying a tray.

"On the contrary, you were quite the heartthrob."

"Then why are you smiling?"

"It's a cute picture."

Aiden slid the tray onto the coffee table. "That's one of the last pictures of us together."

"Why's that?"

"The next week I tore up my knee. Football was over. But it wasn't bad enough to keep me out of the army, so I enlisted." He joined her at the mantel, eyeing the photos. "I needed to get away."

"From what? Your family seems so close, so...perfect."

He raised an eyebrow. "No one's perfect, Nia. But yeah, we were close. I needed out of Echo Mountain, needed to get away from my broken dreams and that look of disappointment on my father's face."

"He probably felt bad *for* you, not disappointed *in* you."

"At that age you don't know the difference. You see it aimed at you and want to get away."

"Did getting away help?"

"A little. Until Dad passed while I was in the sandbox.

Then I had a whole bunch of guilt to deal with." Aiden ran his fingers along the side of the picture frame, as if remembering that very moment. "You know what Dad's passing taught me?"

She shook her head and studied him. He leveled blue eyes at her when he spoke.

"It taught me to shelve the ego and never miss an opportunity to tell someone how you feel."

The room seemed warmer than it was a moment ago. She couldn't break eye contact if she wanted to, yet she didn't really want to. He interlaced his fingers with hers.

Her heart pounded in her ears. He was going to kiss her. She wanted him to kiss her. But this was wrong on so many levels. He was experiencing that syndrome… What was it called? Oh yes, the white-knight syndrome, where a man felt the need to rescue a woman, to be the hero.

"Nia?" he said, his voice soft.

"Yes?"

"May I kiss you?"

She nodded that he could. She treasured this moment, being in this special home, with this special man.

A man she had fallen in love with.

He leaned forward and placed a gentle kiss on her lips. She reached out and gripped his muscled arm, fearing if she didn't hold on to something she might lose her balance.

The kiss was so perfect, so loving, that tears welled in her eyes.

He broke the kiss and leaned back, worry darkening his eyes. "What's wrong?"

"Nothing. Why?" She swiped tears from her eyes. "Oh, right, this, the crying thing. I tend to do that when I'm incredibly…happy."

"You're happy? Wow, I thought I'd lost my touch." He winked. "How about some tea?"

"Sure, I'd love that."

*Love.* She'd said the word, although not in the right context. As if he'd read her mind, he placed another sweet kiss on her lips and went to pour the tea.

As he was about to pour, a scraping sound echoed from the front door.

Aiden grabbed Nia's hand. "Upstairs."

They went quickly to the second floor and darted around the corner. Aiden motioned her into a bedroom.

"No, I'm staying with you," she said.

"Nia—"

The front door swung open with a crash. Heart racing in her throat, she tried to calm herself. Any minute now the house alarm would go off, alerting authorities. Aiden wouldn't have to face the intruders by himself. But how long would it take for help to arrive? She squeezed his hand. He pulled her against his chest, stroking her back.

A few seconds later, they heard a thud.

"Oh, for crying out loud in a bucket," a female voice said.

"It's my sister Cassie," Aiden whispered against Nia's ear.

Aiden took her hand and led them to the top of the stairs. Cassie was in the entryway, the front door open behind her, wrestling with a moving box. The alarm hadn't gone off, since Cassie knew the code to disarm it.

"Need some help?" Aiden asked.

Cassie screamed and stumbled back against the wall. "Jerk! Why do you always do that to me? I could have had a heart attack."

"Sorry," he said.

"No, you're not," Cassie said, still clutching the material of her jacket above her heart. "What are you doing here, anyway? And who's this? Your girlfriend?"

They joined Cassie in the foyer. "Which question do you want me to answer first?" he teased.

Nia liked this lighthearted side of Aiden.

Cassie offered her hand to Nia. "Hi, I'm the sane one in the family, Cassandra McBride."

"Nia Sharpe."

Cassie narrowed her eyes. "Nia, as in the concierge at the resort?"

"That's the one."

"Ooohhh." Cassie nodded and looked from Nia to Aiden.

"Oh, nothing," Aiden said.

Aiden pulled his hand from Nia's and went to close the door.

"Why aren't you at the resort? And where's Mom? Is she okay?" Cassie said.

"Let's see—I'm off for a few days. She's shopping with friends in Victoria, which means she's better than okay." Aiden motioned Nia and Cassie into the living room. "Let's have some tea. Then I'll help you unpack whatever treasures you've dumped into Mom's hallway."

"'Let's have some tea'? Did you really just say that? Since when did you—"

"Since today," Aiden interrupted his sister. He poured tea for Nia and Cassie. "I'll get another cup for myself." He disappeared into the kitchen.

Cassie rocked back and forth on the heels of her sneakers, eyeing Nia. "I like what you've done to my brother."

"I haven't—"

"So…you work at the resort?"

"Yes."

"I hear he's a tough boss."

"He wants things done right."

"So, a real jerk, huh?" She smiled.

"I don't think so. He's always been fair to me."

"Just fair?" She raised an eyebrow.

Nia wasn't sure how much Aiden wanted his family to know about their relationship, or even if the relationship would continue past this current crisis. "Aiden and I have a special friendship," Nia offered.

"Uh-huh."

"Don't grill my friend about me," Aiden said, walking into the room.

*Friend.* He didn't call her his employee this time. Nia had been promoted to friend. Her heart swelled with hope.

"Why not? You're not going to tell me anything." Cassie nodded at Nia. "Good tea, by the way."

"Your brother made it."

Cassie narrowed her eyes at Aiden. "Okay, what's going on? I go away for a few months and Bree finds the love of her life, you've got a girlfriend and Mom's off shopping instead of working on a quilt for church. What's next?"

"Hang around for a while and see," Aiden challenged.

"Maybe I will, to taunt you."

"That's Bree's job," he said. "You're supposed to worship me."

"In your dreams, big guy."

Nia was thoroughly enjoying the family moment. Then her cell buzzed with a text and she glanced at it.

It's Danny. Don't trust anyone. They want u dead 2.

A shudder ran down her spine.

"What is it?" Aiden questioned.

She handed him the phone. He read the message and pressed the power button. "We need to turn our phones off."

"He was trying to warn me," Nia said.

"I understand, but our GPS signals can be tracked if they're on." He switched his phone off, as well. Nia shoved hers into her pocket.

"Wait—what? Who's tracking you?" Cassie asked.

"A drug cartel, federal agents, take your pick," Aiden said.

"Whoa, what kind of trouble did you get yourself into, big brother?"

"It's my fault," Nia said.

"It is not your fault," Aiden corrected her.

"Okay, then it's my brother's fault. He set off this chain of events." Nia addressed Cassie. "He's involved with a drug cartel and came out here to escape, but the trouble followed him."

"Wow. How dangerous?" Cassie said.

Nia cast a worried glance at Aiden.

"It's dangerous," Aiden said. "But we can handle it. Change of subject. Want help with your box?" Aiden asked his sister.

Something crashed through the front window, filling the living room with smoke.

# FIFTEEN

"Get back!" Aiden said.

"What is it?" Nia cried.

Aiden coughed. "Smoke bomb to drive us out of the house." Aiden grabbed a shovel from the fireplace set with one hand and covered his mouth with his shirtsleeve. He scooped up the device. "Get in the basement."

"What about you?"

"Go! If I'm not there in five, get to the barn through the cellar door."

"Where's the basement?" Nia asked a stunned Cassie.

She pointed to the back of the house.

Nia led Cassie out of the living room and away from Aiden. A sinking feeling flooded Nia's chest. No, she wouldn't go there. Aiden would dispose of the smoke bomb and join them in the basement.

Cassie opened the basement door and glanced over her shoulder for her brother.

"He'll be fine," Nia said. "Come on."

They went into the basement and Nia asked, "Is there a way to lock someone out?"

"No."

"Okay, then let's find things to defend ourselves."

As Nia searched a tool bench, she berated herself for assuming trouble wouldn't follow her here.

She berated herself for putting Aiden's life in danger, again.

*Can't think about that now.*

"Did you find anything?" Nia asked.

"This old lamp?" Cassie clutched a metal lamp in her hand.

"Good. Hang on to that." Nia pulled a long screwdriver out of the toolbox and also found a lighter and can of spray paint.

"What are you doing with that?"

"Hopefully nothing, but the threat of setting someone on fire will give us the upper hand. Let's hide."

"Back here." Cassie pointed to the water heater.

Nia turned on her phone and called Nate Walsh for help. "Nate, they found us."

"Where are you?" Nate asked.

"Cassie and I are hiding in the basement, but Aiden's still upstairs."

"On my way."

Nia pocketed her phone and huddled behind the water heater with Cassie.

A few excruciatingly long minutes passed.

"Aiden should be here by now," Cassie said. "It's been more than five minutes. What if they got him? What if they're waiting for us if we go out through the cellar door?"

Nia had to distract an anxious Cassie from going down that dark road, the road that led to despair. If they were forced to defend themselves, they had to be sharp.

"So, what was he like growing up?" Nia said.

"Huh?" Cassie said.

"Aiden."

"Oh, he was a silly guy. He'd always make us laugh."

"I never would have guessed."

"Well, you only know him from work." Cassie paused. "Right?"

Nia shrugged.

"Wow," Cassie said. "So how long have you been dating?"

"We haven't actually been on a date."

"What is wrong with him?"

Absolutely nothing. Even with his gruff manner and short fuse, she thought the man nearly perfect. For her, anyway.

"We've been kind of busy staying out of trouble," Nia said. "But all that will be over soon."

It had to be. She wanted desperately to see what kind of relationship she and Aiden could have outside work.

"Shh, you hear that?" Cassie whispered.

Nia held her breath. Sure enough, floorboards creaked above them. Someone was in the house. Nia gripped the aerosol paint can and lighter, heart pounding in her chest. The footsteps were headed for the basement door.

Nia glanced at the weapons in her hands. The thought of violence turned her stomach, so she motioned Cassie to the cellar door. Nia only hoped the intruder didn't have a partner waiting outside.

As they crossed the room, they heard scuffling up above. Something slammed against the basement door, Cassie squeaked and Nia guided her into the stairwell leading outside. They pushed on the door.

It didn't budge.

"We're trapped," Cassie said.

A crash echoed through the floorboards, then a thud, and three taps, as if someone was banging against the basement door. Nia and Cassie huddled close, waiting, praying.

A loud thud was followed by silence. Nia's heart raced triple time as she clung to Cassie, trying to offer comfort.

The door to the basement creaked open.

"Come on up," Aiden said.

Nia and Cassie shared a look of relief, and then Cassie bolted out of the stairwell and up to the kitchen.

Nia took a breath to calm the adrenaline flowing through her body.

"Oh no, Aiden!" Cassie said.

Panicked, Nia zoomed upstairs. She spotted Aiden on the floor, leaning against the kitchen cabinet clutching his arm. A man lay facedown on the floor. Cassie stood with her hands on her cheeks, looking back and forth from Aiden to the unconscious man.

Nia started to go to Aiden, but he put out his hand. "Tie him up first. Cassie, get the heavy-duty twine out of the top drawer by the microwave."

"Oh, okay, sure." Cassie went to the drawer.

Ignoring Aiden's order, Nia grabbed a dish towel off the counter and rinsed it under cool water. She went to him and knelt down.

"Help Cassie first. Go on," he said.

Nia handed Aiden the towel and went to the unconscious man. That was when she realized she recognized him. "It's the man who broke into my apartment."

"Yeah, Gus Chambers," Aiden said. "But how did he find us?"

"Who cares?" Cassie yanked the man's hands behind his back and started to tie them.

The man suddenly rolled over.

Cassie screamed and stumbled away.

The man started to get up.

Aiden dived at him. "Get out of here!" he ordered the women.

But Nia couldn't move. The guy flipped Aiden onto his back and slugged Aiden's bloodied arm. Aiden's cry lit fury in Nia's chest. She reached under the sink, figuring that was where everyone kept a fire extinguisher.

"No! Stop! Leave him alone!" Cassie screamed.

Nia grabbed the fire extinguisher and turned to see the guy punching Aiden in the face.

And Aiden's arms falling limp to his sides.

Nia charged the attacker, swinging the extinguisher like a baseball bat. It stunned the guy, but didn't stop him. He got to his feet and wavered.

Nia released the pin and got ready to blast him in the face.

"Why wouldn't you talk to me!" Gus shouted, glaring at her. "We could have avoided all this!"

He stumbled as he took a step toward her.

She got ready to fire.

"Freeze," Nate said from the doorway to the living room. "Echo Mountain police."

The room went hauntingly quiet. The ticktock of Mrs. McBride's wall clock echoed across the vinyl flooring.

Gus raised his hands...

Then grabbed a chair and threw it at Nate, who dodged the furniture but didn't fire his gun.

Gus whipped the back door open and rushed outside.

"Echo Mountain police!" another male voice said.

A few seconds of silence rang in Nia's ears, then, "We got him, Nate!"

Cassie collapsed on the floor. "Take care of Cassie," Nia said to Nate as she rushed to Aiden's side. Blood saturated his shirtsleeve and oozed down the side of his face from a cut on his cheek.

"Aiden?" she said.

He didn't respond.

"Aiden?" she tried again. She felt for his pulse. It was steady. Why didn't he open his eyes? Was it blood loss? A concussion?

Nia went to the sink and got another dish towel to clean his wound. When she turned to Aiden, her breath caught. He looked so...broken.

"Ambulance is on the way," Nate said. "Cassie? Cassie McBride, can you hear me?"

"Ya don't have to yell," she said in a weak voice.

"You were unresponsive."

"I'm...I'm okay."

"You don't look okay," Nate said.

"Aren't you the charmer." She started to get up, but her legs gave way and she collapsed against Nate for support.

Nia knelt beside Aiden and wiped blood off his face to determine the severity of his wound.

"You might want to deal with the arm first," Nate offered, holding Cassie against his chest. "Head wounds always bleed like crazy, but his arm shouldn't be bleeding that much."

"Okay, thanks," Nia said.

She spotted a rip in his shirt. She grabbed either end and ripped it wider. Blood seeped from a three-inch gash on his upper arm.

"He's been cut."

"I saw a bloodied knife on the dining room floor," Nate offered.

"I don't know how to—" Nia stopped herself. She would not make excuses. She needed to tend to Aiden, fix him.

But there was so much blood.

Aiden had been sliced and beaten.

Because of her.

"Try to stop the bleeding," Nate prompted gently, jerking her out of her self-recrimination.

"Right." Nia grabbed another towel from a kitchen drawer and wrapped it around Aiden's arm.

"Is he conscious?" Nate asked.

"No."

"Splash some water in his face."

Nia filled a cup with water, went back and sprinkled water on his face with her fingertips. He didn't move.

"Please, my love, open your eyes," she whispered and kissed him.

It was at that moment that she knew, without a doubt, that she was—and probably had been for a while now—deeply in love with Aiden McBride.

She dipped the towel in the water and brushed it across his face, wiping blood from the nasty cut on his cheekbone. His eyelashes fluttered as he opened his normally sky blue eyes, now dulled by pain.

"Welcome back," she said.

"How long have I been out?"

"A few minutes."

"That guy…Gus?" Aiden said.

"Nate got here in time."

"Good, good." He closed his eyes.

"Aiden?" she said.

He opened his eyes. "Wait—did you kiss me?"

She smiled.

"It was nice." He reached for her hand.

She glanced down and noticed blood seeping through the towel on his arm.

"Hang on." She snatched another towel from the drawer. "I hope your mom forgives me for ruining all her towels."

She turned to Aiden.

His eyes were closed. And he was so still.

"Aiden?" she croaked.

"He's lost too much blood," Nate said as he held on to a dazed Cassie.

Chief Washburn rushed into the kitchen from the back. "Everyone okay— Whoa," he said as he caught sight of Aiden.

"He's lost a lot of blood." Nia went to work, bandaging his arm with the fresh towel. It all felt like a dream, more like a nightmare, and she found herself falling into that place of detachment to cope with the situation.

"Officer Carrington and I are taking the suspect into the police station, although we might have to stop by the hospital first."

"Do not let him out of our sight," Nia said, glaring at the chief. "That man is going to pay for what he did to Aiden."

Half an hour later, Nia clutched Aiden's hand as they wheeled him into the emergency room. She was grateful that one of the EMTs was Aiden's cousin, and she let Nia ride along. Whenever Aiden regained consciousness, he would ask for Nia, so her presence seemed to calm him down.

His heart rate was lower than normal, and his cousin Maddie did her best to get him stabilized on the ride to the hospital.

As they wheeled him toward the examining area, a nurse blocked Nia. "I'm sorry, but you can't come in here like that."

Nia glanced at her clothes for the first time since they'd left the house. She was covered in blood from tending to Aiden's injury.

"Nia!" Bree cried, coming into the hospital with Scot by her side. "Are you okay?" She eyed Nia's bloodstained clothes and hands.

"It's Aiden's blood" was all she could say.

"Where is he?"

"They took him in to be examined by a doctor."

"Bree?" Cassie said, entering the ER with Nate by her side.

"What are you doing here?" Bree hugged her sister.

Nia felt suddenly alone. Her only sibling was the reason for all this violence, all this blood. Nia eyed her fingers.

"I came back for an unscheduled visit," Cassie said. "Bad timing on my part."

"What happened?" Bree said.

"Some guy attacked us. Nia saved my life."

The women turned their attention to Nia, who still couldn't look at them.

"She saved Aiden's life, too," Cassie added. "You should have seen her, the way she shoved towels on Aiden's knife wound."

A nurse came out of the examining area and Bree accosted her. "My brother—I need to know how he is."

"They're examining his arm and he may need a CT scan for his head injury. You should relax in the lounge over there. We won't know anything concrete for a while." With a reassuring smile, the nurse walked away.

"Thank you, Nia," Bree said.

Nia glanced down the hall. Bit her lower lip.

"Hey, Cassie, can you wait here for word on Aiden?" Bree said. "I'm going to help Nia get cleaned up."

"I'll wait with her," Nate offered.

"I'm really okay," Cassie said to Nate, who towered over her.

"I believe you," he countered.

"We'll be right back," Bree said to her sister and extended her hand to Nia.

She went to grab it, saw the blood turning her skin brown and snatched her hand back. "I can do it," Nia said.

"I know you can."

Bree accompanied her anyway.

They went into a bathroom and Nia got to work scrubbing the blood off her fingers. Bree stood by, watching. What did she think was going to happen? Did she fear Nia might faint? Have a breakdown?

"You didn't have to come with me," Nia said.

"I wanted to make sure you were okay."

A choke-gasp caught in Nia's throat. "I'm washing your brother's blood off my hands. I'm never going to be okay."

The fear, the pain and the sorrow of the past few hours pounded against Nia like an angry winter storm in Echo Mountain. She struggled to gasp air into her lungs past the ball in her throat, the ball of shame.

"That's it. Let it go." Bree stroked Nia's back as Nia clutched the porcelain sink.

"I thought the violence was behind me, but I'll never get away from it."

"Don't talk like that."

"The way that man beat your brother, he punched and punched, and I couldn't do anything to stop it."

"You had to protect yourself. I'm sure Aiden wanted you to protect yourself."

"Why? He shouldn't care more about me than himself."

"Of course he should. He loves you."

Nia studied Bree's compassionate expression.

"It's obvious, Nia. You bring out the best in each other.

He challenges you to be strong, and you soften his rough edges."

"I also bring him pain and suffering. He deserves better. My stepfather was right. I'm a damaged girl who'll only bring agony to the people in my life."

"Hey! Now, that's enough. I will not stand here and allow you to spew lies. How long are you going to let your stepfather control your life, Nia? Because it sounds like he's still doing it. Is that what you want? Now, finish washing your hands so we can check on Aiden."

Nia glanced at her, ashamed but curious about Bree's firm tone.

Bree shrugged. "Too harsh? I wished someone would have said that to me after I left Thomas and wallowed in shame. I stayed there way too long and don't want to see the same thing happen to you."

"Thanks. I guess you're right."

"Honey, you've seen horrible things tonight, and you're traumatized. Maybe you'll want to see a counselor or talk to Pastor Charles about it. I'm always here, and you know Aiden will be."

Aiden. The image of his bruised and bloodied body threatened to set Nia off on another round of tears. Instead, she glanced at her reflection in the mirror. She wasn't that little girl anymore hiding from her stepdad, avoiding trouble. She was a grown woman who wasn't going to stand for any more abuse. She certainly wasn't going to let Aiden get caught in the cross fire again.

"Whoa, I like that look." Bree leaned against the sink and crossed her arms over her chest.

"This must end."

"What? Not you and Aiden."

"No, my brother's business associates terrorizing me and my friends. It's unacceptable."

"Okay. What are you going to do about it?"

"Find my brother and make him take responsibility for his mistakes."

Nia prayed for guidance in following through with her convictions.

By the time Nia and Bree returned to the waiting area, a small group had formed, including Aiden's mother, a few SAR friends and federal agents Nevins and Parker. As Nia headed for the agents, she noticed Mrs. McBride's worried frown. Nia wouldn't be able to speak to the woman, not until Nia could promise she wouldn't put her children in any more danger.

"Daddy! Daddy!" Claire and Marissa Rankin called.

Nia glanced down the hall and saw Will being pushed in a wheelchair by an orderly. His daughters nearly jumped into his lap.

"Careful, girls," their grandmother said. "Your father's still recovering."

"I'll recover faster with big hugs," Will said.

The girls climbed onto his lap and they shared a group hug. Claire and Marissa giggled, but their grandmother frowned. Their grandfather didn't look too happy, either.

Nia was glad Will was being released. Did that mean he'd recovered his memory? Will smiled, and even though he held his girls in his arms, sorrow dimmed his eyes. Of course, he must have remembered that his wife was dead.

Nia felt a tear trail down her cheek.

"Miss Sharpe?" Agent Nevins said.

She swiped away the tear and turned to him.

"I'm sorry about what happened tonight." He eyed her bloody outfit. "You didn't sustain any injuries, did you?"

"No physical injuries, no. I'm glad you're here. I have an idea that will end this violence once and for all."

"Go on."

"I'm going to use myself as bait to reel in my brother."

# SIXTEEN

Aiden woke up to pure and utter silence. It took him a few seconds to remember where he was. Surrounded by white-and-gray walls, he turned his head toward the light and saw colorful floral arrangements lining the window ledge.

The hospital—they'd taken him to the hospital because he'd been attacked at his mom's house. Panic took hold.

"Nia?" he whispered.

"I'm here," her sweet voice said from the other side of the bed. He turned his head and her adorable face came into focus.

He struggled to smile. "Hi."

"How are you feeling?" she said.

"Loopy, I guess."

"They had you on some pretty strong pain meds."

"For my arm?"

She nodded. "They were worried about the blood loss, so they decided to keep you for observation."

"Are you okay?" he asked.

"Sure, I'm fine."

But he sensed something else behind her answer. He felt her drifting away.

"The guy who attacked me?" he said, needing to know the threat had been neutralized.

"They arrested him. He's not going anywhere this time."

Aiden nodded with relief. Then he remembered something, something he needed to share with Nia. "I have to tell you—"

"You should rest," she said.

"I will, but first I need to tell you something. The strangest thing happened. As that guy was pounding on me, and I fought to stay conscious, you know what I did?"

She shook her head that she didn't.

"I prayed."

Her eyes widened and she took his hand in hers.

"I prayed that you'd be safe," he said. "That even though I'd failed to protect you, you'd somehow escape."

"Nate showed up with the sheriff and another officer."

"And Cassie?"

"She's okay, a little traumatized, but physically okay. She and Bree stayed by your bedside until midnight. I had to go back to the resort and change."

"Aw, I ruined your clothes, didn't I?"

"You didn't ruin anything. I'm so glad you're awake and talking."

"Whoa, never thought I'd hear an employee say those words."

She offered a sad smile and studied their entwined fingers.

"I'm kidding, Nia. You're much more than an employee. You have to know that by now."

She didn't respond.

"Nia?" He shifted in bed and pain shot down his arm to his fingertips. He hissed between clenched teeth.

"I'll get the nurse." She stood.

"No, wait. Stay here and talk to me."

"But—"

"Please?"

She didn't leave, but she didn't reach for his hand again, either.

"What's wrong?" Aiden questioned.

"I guess I'm just exhausted."

There was more to it, but he sensed she didn't want to share.

"Nia?" he pressed.

"This is probably the wrong time to get into this, but—" she glanced at him with regret in her eyes "—whatever happens, I need you to know that I love you, Aiden. With all my heart." She leaned forward and kissed him.

Everything seemed to hurt a little less, and he wanted her to stay close. Instead, she pulled away and refused to make eye contact.

"That felt like goodbye," Aiden said.

"It's not, unless you want it to be."

"I don't understand."

"Is he awake?" Cassie said from the doorway.

"He sure is." Nia motioned his visitors to enter.

Aiden's heart-to-heart conversation with Nia had been interrupted by the women in his family: his sisters Cassie and Bree, and his mom, who carried more flowers and candy into his hospital room.

"Uh, I don't think I'll be here long enough to enjoy the flowers, Mom."

"You'll be here as long as the doctor wants you to be here." She shot a curt nod at Nia.

"Well, I've got to get back to the resort," Nia said.

"No, it's dangerous. What about—"

"It's fine," Nia interrupted Aiden. "I'm working from the cottage and have 24/7 police protection. Work must go on," she said. "Goodbye, everyone." She turned and walked away.

"She is certainly your best employee," his mother said.

"She's much more than that, Mom."

"No kidding," Cassie laugh-snorted.

"She was so upset about everything that happened," Bree said.

"As she should be," his mom snapped. "It's her fault."

"Mother," Aiden said. "Don't talk like that."

"I'm sorry, but Mama Bear goes on the warpath when someone hurts her baby."

"Your baby is thirty-two," Aiden said. "And Nia didn't hurt me."

"It might as well have been her, and I told her so."

"What?" Aiden tried sitting up, but all three women reached out to encourage him to lie down. "Tell me you didn't confront her about this."

"I did."

"Bree, go find her. Bring her back so Mom can apologize."

Bree dashed out of the room.

"I most certainly will not apologize. I wasn't mean, Aiden. I was truthful. You're in danger because of her, and I don't like it."

"But she saved my life, Mom," Cassie said.

"You wouldn't have needed saving if it weren't for Nia and her brother."

Bree jogged back into the room. "She's gone."

Aiden fisted his good hand and pounded the bed.

"It's fine, Aiden," his mom said. "That girl obviously didn't listen to a thing I said, because she sneaked into the hospital and spent most of the night at your bedside."

"Because she loves him, Mom," Bree offered.

"Why can't you kids fall in love with safe, boring people?"

"Mother," Bree admonished.

"Sorry, but you'll never stop being my babies." She glanced at each of them. "Someday you'll understand."

"But none of this is Nia's fault," Bree offered. "Her life's been threatened, too."

"Her only crime is she wouldn't give up on her brother," Aiden said. "Nia spent her childhood protecting her brother from an abusive stepdad and blames herself for not doing enough to keep Danny out of trouble."

"Plus, she blames herself for everything her brother's done, which is *so* not her fault," Bree said.

"But guys, Mom was scared." Cassie took her mom's

hand. "She lost her temper. It's happened to all of us, especially you, Aiden."

"Yeah, well, this was one time when what Nia needed most was love and compassion instead of judgment and criticism."

The room fell silent, so unlike the McBride family.

His mother sighed. "I guess my mama-bear instinct made me lash out at the closest target. I'm sorry, Aiden. Truly, I am."

"I know."

"How about we pray for Nia?" his mom said.

"Yes, I'd like that," Aiden agreed.

The three women looked at him as if he'd sprouted a palm tree out of his head.

"What?" he said.

Bree came in for a big hug.

"Watch the arm," he said.

"Sorry, sorry." She broke the hug and smiled. They all were smiling at him.

"What's wrong with you guys?" he asked.

"Nice to have you back, big brother," Bree said.

And they prayed.

Later that afternoon, after Nia got a few hours' sleep at the cottage, she explained the plan to lure her brother out of hiding to Quinn and Billie, Quinn's fiancée.

"Does Aiden know about this?" Quinn asked.

"No, and I'd like to keep it that way. He needs to focus on recovering."

"Isn't it dangerous?" Billie said.

"Danny's my brother. He's not going to hurt me. But letting his mess drag on is extremely dangerous, not only for me, but also for everyone at the resort."

"It is a busy weekend," Billie said. "But I don't like the thought of you being in harm's way."

"It's my mess to clean up."

"Aiden's not going to be happy when he finds out what you're doing," Quinn said.

"He doesn't have to be happy. He needs to be safe. His mother pointed out that being around me makes that impossible."

"Nia, she was probably riddled with worry about her son," Billie said. "I mean, she's out of town and gets the call that her son's in the hospital. That he was attacked in her home."

"No, she's right," Nia said. "I've continually put him in danger by allowing Aiden to protect me. Now I'll protect both of us."

Billie glanced at Quinn as if she hoped he could say something to change Nia's mind.

"I wish you'd at least talk to Aiden about this," Quinn said.

"Why? I don't need his permission."

"Nia," Billie said. "That's not what he meant."

"I think Aiden's going to be, for lack of a better word, hurt that you've left him out of the loop," Quinn said.

"Maybe, but he'll be hurt worse if he gets it in his head that he's going to be a part of this retrieval plan. I won't put him at risk anymore."

"Because you love him?" Billie said.

Nia glanced at Quinn.

"It's okay," Billie said. "You're not going to lose your job because you fell in love with the boss. It happens to the best of us." She smiled at Quinn, her boss-turned-fiancé. "And I still have my job."

"Until she gets a better one called Mommy," Quinn teased.

A twinge of melancholy arced through Nia's chest at the tender exchange. Quinn and Billie were so blessed to have found each other.

As was Nia, to have found Aiden.

"Well, if we can't talk you out of this—"

"You can't," Nia interrupted Quinn.

"Then I'll put Billie in charge of concierge responsibilities temporarily so you can focus on finding your brother," Quinn said.

"Thank you, both of you," Nia said. "And do me a favor?"

"Sure," Billie said.

"If anything happens to me—"

"Don't talk like that," Quinn said.

"But if it does, can you make sure Aiden knows I never meant to hurt him? That I'm doing this to protect him and my friends in Echo Mountain?"

"We won't have to tell him any such thing because everything's going to be fine," Billie said.

Nia spent the next hour bringing Billie up to speed on the day's events. Nia would stay away from the resort to make sure her brother's business didn't threaten resort guests.

Nia packed her suitcase since she thought it wiser to spend the night in a random hotel rather than on resort property. When Agent Nevins showed up at the cottage, she was ready to go, although she wasn't sure how to proceed with her plan. The last text she got from Danny was from a blocked number, so she wasn't sure how to reach him to set up a rendezvous.

They got into the car. "No Agent Parker today?" Nia asked, not that she minded. He was an aggressive man.

"He'll join us later," Nevins said.

As they pulled out of the resort, she swallowed back the lump in her throat. It was only temporary. She'd be back.

"So, how do we start?" she said.

"Our best bet is to speak to the last person who saw your brother," Agent Nevins said. "Will Rankin."

Poor Will, another victim of her brother's craziness.

"What about the man who attacked Aiden?" she asked.

"Gus lawyered up. He isn't talking."

"Odd, since all he wanted to do was talk to me," she said.

"Don't worry, he'll stay locked up this time—for assault, at least."

Nia nodded. Somehow it didn't make her feel better.

When they arrived at Will's house, his in-laws were reticent to let them in.

"Please, ma'am, it's important that we speak to him as soon as possible to help us close this case," the agent said.

Mrs. Varney debated for a minute. "Fine, we'll take the girls for ice cream."

"Ice cream! Ice cream!" Marissa shouted.

"Me, too," Will said from inside the house.

"You can't, Will. The FBI is here to ask some questions," Mrs. Varney called into the house. "Come on, girls, Grandpa's buying."

Nia heard smacking sounds, which she guessed were the girls kissing their dad goodbye.

"Bring me some volcano chocolate with Gummi Worms," Will called out.

"Eeewww," the girls cried, rushing up to their grandmother at the door.

"Let's go, girls." Their grandmother motioned them outside, where her husband was waiting.

As little Marissa passed, she smiled at Nia. "I know you. You're the lady from the restaurant. You're going to marry my daddy."

Mrs. Varney gasped and glared at Nia.

"Don't worry, Grandma," Claire said. "Marissa thinks everyone is going to marry Daddy."

"Come on, the ice cream's melting." Mrs. Varney quickly shooed the girls away from Nia.

Understandable. Nia had brought trouble to Echo Mountain, and Will had suffered his share.

Nia and Agent Nevins entered the house, where they found Will reclining on the couch.

"Hey, Nia."

"Hi, Will. This is Agent Nevins from the FBI. I'm helping them track down my brother."

"Oh, okay." Will sat up. "How can I help?"

"We need to know everything Danny Sharpe said to you when you fought in the mountains," Agent Nevins said.

"Well, unfortunately, I'm still a little foggy on some stuff."

"Anything could be a huge help," Nia encouraged him.

"Okay, well, he was mostly freaking out about you, Nia. Said the men after him were also after you, and even accused me of being sent to kill him. He wasn't right in the head. I thought maybe he was dehydrated, that he'd been in the mountains too long without water. I tried calming him down, but he whacked me with his gun. I didn't see it coming and I…I'm still a little confused about some things." He glanced at a framed picture of himself, his deceased wife, Megan, and the girls.

It was as if he knew Megan was gone, but he couldn't quite believe it.

"I'm so sorry," Nia said.

Will slowly glanced up. "It's okay. It's all part of the job, right?"

"The job?" Nia said.

"Search and rescue. And man, if anyone needs to be rescued, it's your brother."

"Was he specific about who was after him?" Agent Nevins questioned.

"No, just that he had to save Nia, take her someplace safe."

"Where did you see him?"

"Near Flat Rock Ridge. Aiden would have the specific coordinates."

"But he didn't give you any indication where he was headed?" Nevins asked.

Nia's phone vibrated with a text from an unknown number: Meet me at Spruce Falls.

She shared the text with Agent Nevins. "It must be Danny."

"How far is Spruce Falls?"

"About an hour."

"I'll make arrangements." Agent Nevins excused himself to make some calls.

"Be careful, Nia," Will said. "Your brother seemed pretty confused."

"Yeah, and violent. I am so sorry, Will."

"Stop apologizing. Hey, how's Aiden? I heard he was attacked last night."

"He was, but he's fine. They'll probably release him from the hospital later today."

"Good. I'll have to give him a call."

Nia was about to ask him not to tell Aiden she'd stopped by but thought better of it. Aiden would find out soon enough, and he wouldn't be happy with her decision to use herself as bait.

But the image of a sleeping Aiden, bruised and bandaged, haunted her every waking moment. His mother was right: it *was* Nia's fault that Aiden was stretched out in a hospital bed, so still and fragile-looking.

And Nia knew what she had to do: take responsibility, not blame, and make things right.

His sisters and mother meant well, but they were driving Aiden crazy. As they escorted him back to his cottage on resort property, they hammered him with questions.

"How's your head?" his mom asked.

"Are you dizzy?" Bree questioned.

"What do the stitches look like?" Cassie said.

He opened the door and entered his rustic living room. "Fine, no, and none of your business."

"He's cranky. Get him some pain meds," his mom said.

"He's always cranky," Bree corrected her.

"Am not," he said.

"Are too."

"Enough." His mom intervened.

Although he appreciated them being here, a part of him wanted to be alone. More specifically, he wanted to see Nia to make sure she was safe.

"I don't know why you won't come back to the farm for dinner," his mom said. "Harvey fixed the window, and he and my Bible-study group cleaned up the place, although I took care of the kitchen myself. It was a mess."

Yeah, mostly from Aiden's blood. He suddenly realized how traumatic this must have been for his mother.

"Hey, Mom, I'm sorry." He eased himself onto the sofa, his arm secured against his body in a sling.

"You should be sorry. Now I have to drive all the way home to make dinner and drive all the way back to serve it to you."

"You could use my kitchen," Bree offered.

"Or I could order from the resort kitchen," Aiden said. "I'm a grown man."

"That's debatable," Bree said.

His mom motioned to Bree. "Let's go to your place and whip something up for dinner. Cassie, you stay here and watch over your brother."

Good. It would give him a chance to call Nia.

Scott and Quinn stepped into the doorway.

"Hey, honey," Scott said to Bree. "Where are you going?"

"Making dinner for the prince."

"Hey!" Aiden protested.

"If the crown fits," Bree called as she and his mom left.

Scott and Quinn joined Aiden in the cottage.

"How are ya doing, boss?" Scott said.

"Better than last night."

"How many stitches?"

"Twenty-two," Cassie offered.

"I've got good news," Quinn said. "The guest complaints were generated by one IP address, so it was like I suspected. Someone was messing with you, Aiden."

"That is good news, I guess. Hey, have either of you seen Nia?"

Quinn glanced at Scott, then back at Aiden.

"What?" Aiden said.

"She's gone," Quinn said.

"Gone? Gone where?"

"To help the feds find her brother."

# SEVENTEEN

It felt as if he'd been punched in the gut, only this time with a baseball bat. Aiden sucked in a breath and fought back his temper, which was about to explode in front of his friend, boss and baby sister.

"Uh-oh, I know that look," Cassie said. "I'm going to go help Mom make dinner." Cassie dashed out of the cottage.

"I told her to talk to you about it first," Quinn said.

"Agent Nevins probably manipulated her."

"I don't think so," Quinn said. "It sounded like it was her idea."

Quinn leaned against the refrigerator across the room, and Scott sat at the kitchen table.

"If she's got the feds protecting her, she'll be fine," Scott offered.

"I don't trust them," Aiden said.

"Why not?" Quinn asked.

"They've been pressuring Nia from the beginning about her brother, even though it's clear that she doesn't know anything."

"Maybe she does," Scott offered.

"What are you talking about?" Aiden snapped.

Scott put out his hand in a calming gesture. "Before you bite my head off, let's think about this. What if her brother gave her something, or told her something that could lead the feds to his location?"

"And you've got to wonder, why is the guy still hanging around?" Quinn said. "Because he's worried about his sister, or is it something else?"

"The only thing that would keep a guy like that around is money," Scott said.

"Like the two hundred thousand he stole from the drug cartel," Aiden added. "Why hasn't he taken it and fled the state?"

"Maybe he really is worried about putting his sister in danger and wants her to go with him," Quinn said.

"She'd never go," Aiden countered.

Quinn raised an eyebrow. "Unless she thought it would protect the man she loves."

Aiden stood up and grabbed his jacket. "I've got to find her."

"Take it easy," Quinn said. "You're wounded."

"I'm fine."

Quinn didn't move.

"Would you let twenty-two stitches stop you from finding Billie before she disappeared with her criminal brother?" Aiden challenged.

Quinn sighed. "Point taken. Let's go to my office and see if we can ping her cell-phone location."

Forty-five minutes later, Nia and the two federal agents were approaching Talus Ridge. The falls were less than a quarter of a mile away. This was truly almost over. She wondered if that meant she'd get her life back.

Deep in her heart, she feared things could never go back to the way they were. Everyone knew now. They knew about her criminal brother, her shame, and worse, how she'd put people she cared about in horrible danger.

No, after they arrested Danny, she'd quietly slip out of town. It would be better that way, even for Aiden.

Especially for Aiden.

"How far?" Agent Nevins said.

Agent Parker had remained oddly quiet.

"About ten minutes," she said. Thankfully, the ankle

brace Dr. Spence suggested she wear gave her the support she needed on this moderate hike.

"As we get closer, we're going to hang back so your brother doesn't get spooked and take off," Agent Nevins said. "If you can get him to say anything about stealing the money, or killing the other agents, that's even better."

Sadness washed over her. She'd gone from being her brother's protector to betraying him. Yet, at this point, she wasn't sure he was capable of making the best decisions for himself.

"Here, you'll need this." Agent Nevins handed her a small device. "Press the red button to record your conversation."

The device was black and about the size of a thumb drive. She slipped it into her lightweight jacket pocket.

*God, I hope I'm doing the right thing.*

They reached the last switchback before the falls and headed down toward the water. Nia loved this place because she could get so close to the falls. Some people even swam in the water.

"Okay, this is a good place for you to hang back," she said.

"We'll stay close enough to protect you."

"I'm not worried. He won't hurt me."

She continued down the trail, secretly hoping he'd deny knowing anything about the stolen money or the dead federal agents. Even though she told herself she'd given up on her brother, a part of her never would. A part of her would always think of him as that little kid with the messy brown hair who loved collecting baseball cards and playing soccer.

As she approached the water, she scanned the area.

"Danny?" she called out.

She carefully stepped on the wet rocks to make her way to a bigger rock in the middle of the pool of water. She wanted him to see her, to feel safe enough to come out.

Something caught her eye and she turned a little too

suddenly. Her foot slipped out from under her and she plunged into the water. Stunned by the frigid temperature, she gasped before she went under.

Flailed her arms to stay above the surface.

But her pack was weighing her down.

She broke through the surface and reached for a rock, but she couldn't get ahold of it.

She heard a splash and suddenly her brother was in the water, pushing her up onto the rocks.

"Are you okay?" Danny asked, shifting beside her.

"I'm embarrassed." She sat up and eyed herself. "And soaked."

"You look like a soggy cat." He squeezed water from his shirt.

"Thanks for saving me."

"You would have made it out eventually." He eyed her. "But it's nice to save you for a change."

Suddenly she realized he seemed perfectly fine, not crazy or out of his mind.

"What's going on, Danny?" She automatically felt for the recording device but realized it wouldn't work after being submerged. Relief washed over her.

Danny must have noticed her movement. "What've you got for me?" he teased. "Soggy chocolate?" He reached into her pocket.

"Danny—"

He pulled out the recording device.

"What...what's going on?"

"I wasn't going to use it."

He glanced at the device, then at the surrounding woods. "Nia, what did you do?"

"I'm sorry."

Danny jumped to his feet and whipped out a gun.

A crack echoed through the falls.

Danny dropped the gun, gripped his shoulder and fell back into the water.

"No!" Nia launched herself toward her brother and grabbed him by the shirt collar before he sank into the water.

Agent Parker came up behind her.

"Help me!" she demanded.

The agent pulled Danny up onto the rocks.

"Danny, Danny, open your eyes," she pleaded.

His eyes fluttered open. "Why…why did you—"

"Where's the money, Sharpe?" Agent Parker got in Danny's face.

"You didn't have to shoot him."

"He was about to shoot you," Nevins said from ten feet away, still holding his firearm.

"No, he wasn't." She pulled off her backpack and searched for dry socks in a sealed plastic bag. She pulled them out and shoved them against Danny's gunshot wound.

"The money!" Parker demanded, grabbing Danny's hair.

"Stop it!" Nia shoved Agent Parker aside. "We've got to call search and rescue." Nia continued to put pressure on Danny's wound.

"I don't suppose you recorded anything," Nevins said.

"The device was damaged when I fell into the water. You can interrogate him when we get back."

"We don't have time for that," Parker said.

She heard a click against her ear. He was pointing a gun at her temple. She froze and automatically put up her hands. Danny's eyes widened with fear.

"I'll kill your sister if you don't tell us where the money is," Parker said.

"And admit to killing Agents Brown and McIntyre," Nevins said.

"You know I didn't kill them," Danny protested.

"What are you doing?" Nia said, more irritated than scared by their aggressive tactics.

"We're closing this case," Nevins said. "That's what you want, isn't it? If you can get your brother to tell us where the money is, maybe we won't add *your* murder to his list of felonies."

Danny studied Nia's eyes and shook his head. "If I tell them, we're both dead."

"And if you don't, just your sister dies," Nevins snapped.

"It's okay, Danny," Nia said. "I forgive you."

Parker snapped the gun back and stood. "What's wrong with you, woman? Get him to tell us—"

Two shots rang out.

Nia shrieked.

Agent Parker gripped his chest. With a stunned expression, he fell into the water.

She struggled to make sense of what was happening. Agent Nevins had just killed his partner.

A few seconds later, Nevins pressed the barrel of his gun against the back of her head. "Where's the money?"

If this was Nia's last moment on earth, she wanted to be focused on love and beauty, not violence and fear. She interlaced her fingers in prayer.

"Don't do that," Nevins said.

"You can kill me, but you can't tell me how to die."

A gunshot echoed across the falls.

"This is the police! Put the gun down!" a man called.

Nevins grabbed Nia's arm.

"Let her go!" the policeman called.

Nevins started to pull her to her feet.

Two shots echoed across the water.

Nevins's fingers sprang free of her arm and she collapsed against Danny. Her body trembled violently.

"Spike, get him out of the water," a man said. She recognized the voice as Deputy Nate Walsh. "Doc, check on the brother. Harvey, get the litter ready. I'll check on the other agent."

It sounded as if help had arrived in time, yet she couldn't stop trembling.

"Nia? It's Dr. Spencer. May I examine your brother?"

She nodded affirmative, unable to peel her body off of Danny.

Nia felt a hand squeeze her shoulder.

"Sweetheart?" The sound of Aiden's voice made her breath catch. "You've done a great job protecting your brother, but now let the doc take a look, okay?"

As she pushed away from Danny, Aiden pulled her against his chest and rocked slightly.

"They shot Danny," she said.

"I know, honey, I know."

"I think…I think they were setting him up."

"Don't think about that now. The police will figure it out. Shh."

She sobbed against him, realizing how utterly foolish she'd been to think she could leave this man, a man who, even with stitches in his arm and a mild concussion, had come out to rescue her.

"You shouldn't be here," she said.

"Ah, still micromanaging, I see."

"Your arm."

"It's fine. We're all fine."

"My brother…?"

"Doc?" Aiden said.

"Through and through. She did a good job of stopping the bleeding. He should be okay, but he needs a hospital."

"Let's get him on the litter," Harvey said.

"Honey, they need space to work." Aiden guided her to a rock a few feet away. "Hang on while I get you a blanket."

Hugging herself against the chill, she watched him whip off his pack and dig inside, one-handed. Yet somehow he managed to find a dry blanket and draped it across her shoulders.

"I fell in," she uttered.

"I can see that," he said with what sounded like amusement in his voice.

"How did you find me?"

"Tracked your cell phone. Then Will called, filled me in on your plan."

"Are you upset with me because I agreed to help the agents?"

"The only thing that matters is that you're alive."

Nate felt for Agent Parker's pulse and glanced at Nia and Aiden. He shook his head, indicating that the agent was gone.

Nia bit back a gasp. How foolish she'd been to trust these men. "I thought...I thought it was the best way—" she glanced up "—to protect you."

"Shh." He pulled her against his chest and stroked her back. "You're okay. It's all over now."

Later that day, Nia sat beside her brother's hospital bed, wishing he'd open his eyes. Apparently so did the local authorities. Nate Walsh stayed close, as did Aiden.

Aiden kept trying to convince her to get checked out by a doctor, but she knew she wasn't hurt physically. Emotionally, on the other hand...

It was going to take a while to forget all that had happened, to wipe away the images of her brother's bloody shoulder, Aiden's bloody arm and the feel of a gun pressed against her head.

Danny moaned and opened his eyes.

"Hey, little brother. You're awake."

"Are you okay?" he said.

"Me? You're the one in a hospital bed."

He reached out to hold her hand, but his wrist was handcuffed to the bed.

She slipped her fingers through his. "Are you up to talking to the police?"

"No, no way. Never."

"Danny—" she squeezed his hand "—I trust these people."

"Cops lie. Those federal agents were going to kill you."

"Yes, but Deputy Nate Walsh saved our lives today. I think you should give him a chance."

"They're going to pin the murders of those first two agents on me. I didn't kill anyone."

"If you tell the truth, they'll believe you," Nia said.

"You're too trusting."

"Please?"

"Fine."

Nia went into the hallway and motioned to Nate. "He's awake."

Nate, Chief Washburn and Aiden joined her in the hospital room. Aiden offered a curt nod as he passed. What was that about?

"We'd like to take your official statement, Danny," the chief said.

"I was duped."

"Please explain," Nate said.

"Back in Detroit, I got into some—" he glanced at Nia "—some trouble with a drug operation. The two feds that arrested me said if I helped them they'd give me immunity."

"Those feds being Nevins and Parker?"

"Yeah. They were on a special task force to weed out corrupt agents. They wanted me to steal a few grand from my boss, who they claimed was working with them."

"Federal agents working with a drug cartel?" the chief scoffed.

"I know, I'm an idiot, but they were offering me a deal to stay out of jail, so I'd pretty much believe anything."

"What happened next?" Nate asked.

"My job was a deliveryman, so I picked up a messenger bag but didn't deliver it. Brown and McIntyre were supposed to arrest me. When the cash went missing, that would be Nevins's evidence they were dirty. But I didn't get arrested, and the bag had way more than a couple of grand inside. Then people started trying to kill me."

"Oh, Danny," Nia said, touching his hand.

"What people?" Nate asked.

"My boss, Parker and Nevins, take your pick. So I ran. Hitched my way out here to see Nia. I guess they assumed she was in on it, or she'd launder the money through the resort or something. I don't know. I thought about shipping the money back to my boss, but what if someone else opened the package and kept it for himself? I figured the money was my only leverage. I didn't know what to do." He sighed. "I watched Nia take off into the mountains and I followed her. When I saw Brown and McIntyre go after her, I fired off a few shots to scare them away but I didn't shoot them, honest."

Nia glanced at Aiden. "That must have been the gunshots we heard."

He nodded.

"But not the gunshots that killed Agents Brown and Mc-Intyre," Nate said.

"Gus Chambers probably shot them," Danny said. "He's muscle for the Detroit operation."

"And he came to retrieve the money?" the chief said.

Danny nodded.

"But why kill two federal agents?" the chief asked.

"Unless Gus didn't kill them," Nate offered. "It's more likely Parker and Nevins shot the other agents. After speaking with the FBI, I got the impression Agents Brown and McIntyre were suspicious of Parker and Nevins, so Parker and Nevins wanted them out of the way. Plus, if they pinned the murders on Danny, that would turn up the heat."

"Right, so more law enforcement would be on the lookout for him," the chief said.

"Once they found him, he'd be arrested for murder." Nia squeezed Danny's hand.

"And no one would believe my word against a cop's."

The room fell silent as they all digested Danny's story.

"So, where is the money?" the chief asked.

Danny looked away.

"Danny, these are the most trustworthy men I know," Nia said.

He sighed. "At the cottage."

"Bree's cottage? With the golden retriever?" Nia asked.

"Yeah."

"Why there?"

"I was going to stash it at your apartment that first night, but your boss showed up. Then I heard Gus was in town and didn't want to give him a reason to come after you. I needed to stash it in a place they couldn't trace back to me."

"How did you get into her cottage?" Aiden said.

Danny glanced at Nia. "I sneaked into the house the day I texted you to meet at the restaurant. I was going to sneak in after you left, but when the dog escaped and you ran after it, that's when I went inside and hid the money. You came back into the house and almost caught me, so I hid until you left."

"That must have been what set off the alarm," Aiden said.

"So, where's the money now?" Nate asked.

"I hid it behind a dresser upstairs."

"I'll get on it," the chief said.

The next few days were a blur. The FBI had Danny under constant protection, and by Wednesday he was well enough to be released from the hospital. He'd agreed to go back to Detroit, where the FBI would question him further. The hope was if he cooperated and told them everything he knew about the drug gang, they'd dismiss the original charges brought by Nevins and Parker.

It was hard saying goodbye to her brother, but she felt as if he was finally on the right track.

She glanced at the mended Peace figurine Aiden had left on her desk. Unfortunately, she didn't feel as if she and Aiden had gotten back on track. Since she'd returned to work, Aiden had been polite and businesslike yet kept his distance, like before…

Before they'd kissed, before she'd told him she loved him.

That day at the falls when he'd said it was all over, had he meant their relationship was over, as well?

No, that was the one good thing that had come out of this violent mess: she and Aiden had admitted their feelings for one another.

How did that suddenly disappear?

"Daydreaming at work, Miss Sharpe?" Aiden said from her doorway.

"Oh, hi."

"Did your brother get off okay?"

"He did."

"Good. I'm glad." He stepped into her office and placed a folder on her desk. "Some vendor inquiries about Independence Day weekend events. Please narrow down that list by the end of the day tomorrow." He turned to leave.

"What's wrong?" she said.

He hesitated, then turned to her. "I'm sorry?"

"You're not talking to me."

"Aren't we talking right now?"

"You know what I mean."

He glanced at the floor but didn't respond.

"Are you angry because I worked with the agents to bring in my brother?" she asked.

"I'm not angry." He hesitated. "I'm disappointed."

Her heart sank. "In me?"

"In the choice you made not to share your decision with me."

"I didn't need your permission."

"That's not the point. Couples, partners, rely on each other equally. That doesn't seem to be happening here, between us. You rely on yourself, and you shut me out—"

"I wanted to protect you."

"Nia, every time you keep something from me, something potentially life threatening, you're basically reminding me how broken I am."

Nia stood abruptly. "Don't say that. I've never thought of you as broken. Ever."

"Actions speak for themselves."

"Aiden—"

"I've got work to do. If you'd like to take a few days off to recover from the past week, I'd completely understand."

He left her office and closed the door.

Aiden stood in the hallway for a good five seconds. He'd done it. He'd said what was on his mind. Not easy for a guy who usually kept his feelings bottled up inside.

He headed for his office, but instead of going in, he went outside to get some fresh air, to think.

He loved Nia. No doubt about it. And maybe she loved him. But theirs had to be an equal love, the kind of love that encouraged honesty, respect and trust. He'd been honest about how he felt. He knew that was the only way to see if a relationship had the foundation it needed to survive the trials of life.

They'd already experienced their share of trials. You'd think after everything they'd been through, their relationship would be stronger. Perhaps it could be, but not if she continued to protect him. He hoped he'd gotten through to her, that she understood where he was coming from and how he got here.

What happened next was totally up to Nia. In the meantime, he'd put up the wall and be his usual gruff self. After all, he may have lost Nia, but he was still manager of the resort.

When Nia stopped by Bree's for a quick visit, she found Bree and Scott having coffee with Nate Walsh.

Bree led Nia into the kitchen and poured her a cup of coffee, as well. "Nate was filling us in on Gus Chambers."

"They'll deal with him back in Detroit," Nate said. "He

still claims he wasn't out to hurt you, Nia, that he wanted to pick your brain about your brother."

"He sliced Aiden with a knife," Nia countered.

"Says he was trying to intimidate Aiden into stepping aside, but Aiden charged him."

"My brother." Bree shook her head.

"Hey, your brother is a hero in my book," Scott said.

"I still can't believe Agent Nevins killed his partner," Nia said.

"He was going to pin that murder on your brother," Nate offered. "It looks like Parker wasn't dirty, but Nevins needed him dead so Nevins could recover the money himself. Nevins could claim Danny killed Parker, so Nevins had to kill Danny, but Danny never confessed the whereabouts of the money."

"So Nevins traded his integrity for a couple hundred grand," Scott said.

"Actually, it turns out there was more than two hundred grand in Danny's bag. It was closer to half a million bucks, but he claims he didn't know that. Anyway, I'd better get back." Nate stood and glanced at Bree. "How's your sister doing?"

"I think she's okay, although she's not asking as many questions as usual."

"She might have nightmares for a while," Nate said. "Get her to talk about them. That usually helps."

"Okay, thanks."

"I'll walk you out," Scott said. "Gotta get back to work anyway." He kissed Bree on the cheek.

"Later, handsome," Bree said.

The men left the cottage and Bree cracked a playful smile.

"What's with the smile?" Nia said.

"Methinks Deputy Nate has a crush on my little sister." She sat at the table and sighed. "Love is in the air."

"For some of us," Nia muttered.

"Okay, what's up, girlfriend?"

Nia didn't intend to complain about Aiden, but Bree kept pushing.

"Aiden didn't approve of my decision to work with the feds," Nia said.

"And now he's, what? Ignoring you?"

"No, it's not like that. But he's closed himself off again."

"What does that look like? I'm curious."

"He avoids eye contact, keeps his physical distance, and he shuts down every time I'm near him. It's like his thoughts are locked in his mind fortress, and he's not letting me in." She stood and paced to the window. "We grew so close during the last week. We know things about each other, personal things. But now it's like I'm back to being an employee, nothing more. He accused me of shutting him out, yet he's doing the same thing to me."

"And how does that feel?"

Nia spun around. "Horrible. It's like he doesn't care about my feelings. I mean, how could he…?" Her voice trailed off.

The anger and frustration, the gut-wrenching pain of being shut out by Aiden was exactly what Aiden must have felt when he found out she'd decided to help the agents find her brother, without talking to Aiden first.

"Nia?" Bree said.

"I think I get it. I understand how he felt." She let the wave of emotions wash over her: the shame and hurt of being excluded.

"What do I do now?" Nia said. "I love him so much."

"Well—" Bree crossed her arms over her chest "—love is awesome, but it has its challenges. Like being honest with one another. It sounds like Aiden was honest with you today. Are you willing to do the same?"

Aiden locked up the barn and headed for his cottage. The SAR meeting had gone well, although his mind was only half in the game tonight.

He couldn't stop thinking about Nia. Would she accept

his offer and take a few days off work? He'd miss her if she did. Sure, he kept his distance, but he always felt better when he knew she was on resort property.

"You have to stop doing that," he grumbled.

He had to stop thinking about her, wondering how she was doing, if she had nightmares from the shooting at Spruce Falls. He missed her so much, even though she worked in the same building. What a mess.

"Hey," Nia said.

He glanced up and noticed her sitting in a chair on the front porch of his cottage.

"I'm sorry. Did I miss a meeting?" he asked.

"Nope." She stood and approached him.

"Are you okay?"

"I will be." She looped her hands around his neck and kissed him.

Her lips were warm and soft and tasted of cinnamon. She broke the kiss and said, "You're right. It feels horrible."

"W-w-what?"

She smiled. "No, not the kiss. That was lovely. I meant, being shut out feels horrible." She released him and took a few steps away. "At the time I made the decision to shut you out, I couldn't get an image out of my head." She turned to him. "The image of you lying in the hospital bed with a bandaged arm and a bruised face. And it was my fault."

"Nia—"

"Don't interrupt. This baring-of-the-soul thing is terrifying, and I could very possibly run away so I won't have to finish."

He cracked a slight smile. She was absolutely adorable. "Go on."

"I've been trained since childhood to take care of other people, on my own, in silence." She sighed. "But if you decide to give me another chance at this partner thing, well, I'll promise to include you in my decision making, even if I think you'll disapprove."

"We won't always agree on everything. That's life."

"True. And we may not agree on this, but I'll always protect you, Aiden. That's what I do for the people I love."

"I am so blessed to be on that list."

"You're at the top of that list, my love."

"There's no place I'd rather be." He pulled her into his arms and kissed her.

\* \* \* \* \*

*Look for more books in*
*Hope White's* ECHO MOUNTAIN *miniseries*
*later in 2015. You'll find them wherever*
*Love Inspired Suspense books are sold!*

Dear Reader,

Have you ever felt as if experiences from your past continue to make you question your decisions in the present? Life is full of lessons, personal growth and even regrets, and some people struggle with those regrets a bit longer than necessary.

In *Payback*, Aiden regrets the harsh words he shared with his father the last time they spoke, and Nia regrets not being able to help her brother make better decisions about his life. Yet everyone has his or her own journey, and hopefully, through faith, friendship and prayer, we make our way through life challenges toward peace.

Thanks to Nia's compassion and love, Aiden learns self-forgiveness, and Aiden helps Nia accept that she's not responsible for her brother's mistakes, mistakes that put her life in danger.

Throughout the course of their story, Nia and Aiden learn to appreciate each other's desire to protect the people they love. They also learn how to let go—of their personal regrets, their fear of intimacy and their need to control everything around them.

I hope you enjoy their journey as a couple, as they grow in their faith, and learn to embrace the blessing of love.

Peace,
*Hope White*

# COMING NEXT MONTH FROM
## Love Inspired® Suspense

### Available July 7, 2015

## DETECTING DANGER
*Capitol K-9 Unit* • by Valerie Hansen
The criminal Daniella Dunne once testified against is now free
and setting off bombs around town. When Daniella's witness
protection identity is compromised, she turns to capitol K-9 unit
officer Isaac Black to prevent the explosive situation that's looming.

## JOINT INVESTIGATION
*Northern Border Patrol* • by Terri Reed
A serial killer is on the loose, and Canadian Mountie Drew Kelley
and FBI agent Sami Bennett reluctantly combine forces to bring
the madman to justice. Chasing the killer across their nations'
borders, Drew vows to protect his attractive partner at all costs.

## EMERGENCY REUNION • by Sandra Orchard
After Sherri Steele is attacked in her ambulance, deputy
Cole Donovan insists on safeguarding the stubborn paramedic.
But when his brother becomes a suspect, he must choose
between the love of his former crush or duty to his family.

## HIGH-RISK HOMECOMING • by Alison Stone
When Ellie Winters discovers someone is running drugs
through her new shop, FBI agent Johnny Rock is called in.
Can the charming lawman from her past keep Ellie safe, or
will her homecoming become short-lived?

## HIDDEN IDENTITY • by Carol J. Post
Meagan Berry faked her death to escape an abusive
relationship, but now the violent man has found her. Meagan
must turn to handsome cop Hunter Kingston to keep her from
an early grave.

## HEADLINE: MURDER • by Maggie K. Black
Daniel Ash thought his days as a bodyguard were behind
him, but he's thrown right back into the field when journalist
Olivia Brant's investigative skills place her—and him—in a
crime gang's sights.

---

LISCNM0615

# REQUEST YOUR FREE BOOKS!

## 2 FREE RIVETING INSPIRATIONAL NOVELS
## PLUS 2 FREE MYSTERY GIFTS

*Love Inspired®*

# SUSPENSE

### RIVETING INSPIRATIONAL ROMANCE

*Love Inspired®*

# Love the Love Inspired book you just read?

**Your opinion matters.**

**Review this book on your favorite book site, review site, blog or your own social media properties and share your opinion with other readers!**